"You've found

"and take care of the horses.

"Only because I have to." Trent's defensive tone was hiding something. "Not by choice."

"You're doing a good job."

"Not really." Trent faced her then and met her gaze. "I can't seem to turn it off."

"You're juggling a lot. I, for one, think you're handling it all well." Gracie began placing equal amounts of candy in each girl's basket. But she felt Trent's stare and glanced up. The intensity in his gaze lifted the hair on her arms.

"Thank you," he said. "For the encouragement, for coming over and for everything you're doing with the girls. They're happy. It's because of you."

Heat rose up her neck. "They're easy to love. I enjoy my time with them."

Her eyes met his, and they shared a moment of understanding...and more. The way he was staring made her wonder if he ever thought of her romantically. She'd been thinking of him romantically. Way too often.

Jill Kemerer writes novels with love, humor and faith. Besides spoiling her mini dachshund and keeping up with her busy kids, Jill reads stacks of books, lives for her morning coffee and gushes over fluffy animals. She resides in Ohio with her husband and two children. Jill loves connecting with readers, so please visit her website, jillkemerer.com, or contact her at PO Box 2802, Whitehouse, OH 43571.

Books by Jill Kemerer

Love Inspired

Wyoming Legacies

The Cowboy's Christmas Compromise
United by the Twins
Training the K-9 Companion
The Cowboy's Christmas Treasures
The Cowboy's Easter Surprise

Wyoming Ranchers

The Prodigal's Holiday Hope
A Cowboy to Rely On
Guarding His Secret
The Mistletoe Favor
Depending on the Cowboy
The Cowboy's Little Secret

Visit the Author Profile page at LoveInspired.com for more titles.

THE COWBOY'S EASTER SURPRISE

JILL KEMERER

LOVE INSPIRED
INSPIRATIONAL ROMANCE

LOVE INSPIRED®
INSPIRATIONAL ROMANCE

ISBN-13: 978-1-335-93709-4

The Cowboy's Easter Surprise

Copyright © 2025 by Ripple Effect Press, LLC

Recycling programs
for this product may
not exist in your area.

For questions and comments about the quality of this book, please contact us
at CustomerService@Harlequin.com.

® is a trademark of Harlequin Enterprises ULC.

Love Inspired
22 Adelaide St. West, 41st Floor
Toronto, Ontario M5H 4E3, Canada
www.LoveInspired.com

Printed in Lithuania

MIX
Paper | Supporting
responsible forestry
FSC® C021394

Shouldest not thou also have had compassion
on thy fellowservant, even as I had pity on thee?
—*Matthew* 18:33

Thank you to all the authors of the children's books I devoured as a kid. You made me fall in love with reading and helped nurture my imagination to tell stories of my own.

Chapter One

Trent Lloyd sensed mutiny in the air.

If he didn't ask any questions, there was a slim chance he'd avoid whatever headache his three nieces were preparing to hit him with from the back seat of his truck. One by one, the trio buckled their seat belts. *Click, click, click.* The snowy weather couldn't be more miserable for a Monday in the third week of March. That was Jewel River, Wyoming, for you, though—harsh winters were the norm. Trent checked the rearview mirror as he backed out of the babysitter's driveway.

Three blondes with different shades of blue eyes met his gaze in the mirror. None of them looked happy.

Nine-year-old Emma sat directly behind him, four-year-old Noelle was kicking her legs from the booster seat in the middle and seven-year-old Sadie sat in a matching booster seat on the other side of Noelle.

"We aren't going back there. The three of us decided." Emma tended to assume responsibility for her younger sisters. Sadie was more reserved, but her brain never stopped processing information. And little Noelle had Trent wrapped around her pinkie finger and tied into a tight bow. All three of them did, really.

The girls had been living with him for over a week, and his carefully ordered life had been turned inside out and upside down, leaving him thoroughly shaken.

He flicked on the windshield wipers and checked for on-coming traffic before pulling onto the road. Should he ask Emma why? He wasn't thrilled with Mrs. Pine, either, but at this point, she was the only person willing to watch Noelle while the other two were in school. After school, Emma and Sadie joined Noelle at Mrs. Pine's, and Trent picked them up at five.

"I don't like her!" Noelle's outburst held a tint of fear, and he inwardly sighed at the tears sure to be on their way. "She's mean."

No point in arguing. Mrs. Pine didn't seem to enjoy children much for being a full-time babysitter.

"She spanked Sammy, and he didn't do anything." Emma huffed. "He's only three. That kid cried and cried. Gave Sadie a headache."

"My head does hurt, Uncle Trent." Sadie's small, pitiful voice made his gut clench. Not Sadie, too. He glanced back again. Sure enough, his middle niece was on the verge of tears. Noelle reached over to hold Sadie's hand.

"And she smokes surrogates." Noelle's lower lip plumped out. "It's yucky."

"Cigarettes, Noelle," Emma said sharply. "She smokes cig-arettes."

"Well, I don't like 'em! They stink. Make me wanna throw up."

Mrs. Pine smoked? Trent grimaced. This wasn't a good development. His brother—technically his stepbrother—would not be okay with the girls being exposed to second-hand smoke. Nor would Kevin allow the girls to be physically disciplined by anyone but himself.

None of this was sounding good.

Trent focused on making his way down Center Street as the snow continued to fall. At ten minutes past five, daylight had already begun to fade. The huge rambling farmhouse he called home was only a few minutes away. Not having to pay for housing was just one of the many perks of being the manager of Moulten Stables. The house stood directly across the road from the horse-boarding operation. When he'd accepted the job last summer, he'd had no idea the six bedrooms would come in so handy.

"I'm telling Daddy," Emma said. "He won't like it."

Trent bit his tongue. She was correct. Kevin wouldn't like it, but Emma wouldn't be able to talk to her father for some time. His highly classified government job—one that didn't technically exist on paper—was the reason the girls were living with Trent. Kevin had been assigned on a special mission for twelve—possibly eighteen—months. The covert operation meant Trent had no idea where his brother was or what he was doing. While Kevin had assured him he'd do everything in his power to FaceTime the girls every other Sunday afternoon, Trent knew it wouldn't always be possible.

Kevin needed him to raise the girls in his absence, and Trent would do anything for his brother and his nieces. They were his family. The girls' mother had died two years ago from breast cancer. Raising them here in Jewel River was a small price to pay while their dad saved the world. Unfortunately, their arrival had created hiccup after hiccup— none their fault—but he continued to deal with the fallout nonetheless.

If the girls refused to go to Mrs. Pine's, where did that leave him? Out of options. That's where. "We'll talk about it when we get home."

"We'll come to the stables after school." Emma had the confidence of a general victorious in war. Trent wouldn't mind borrowing some of her bravado. But the stables? Terrible idea.

Noelle couldn't hang out in a cold barn all day with him,

and the other two weren't suited to stay there after they got out of school. They had homework to do, snacks to eat and they needed to be in a warm home, not surrounded by hay and horses.

"I'll bring blankie, Uncle Trent." Noelle didn't go anywhere without her pink blankie. "Mrs. Pine won't hide blankie ever again."

Ah, so that was one of the problems. Maybe he could talk to the babysitter about how important the blanket was to Noelle. And ask her not to smoke. And tell her she wasn't allowed to spank the girls.

He inwardly groaned. Put like that, the woman had a lot of strikes against her.

He turned into the driveway and parked the truck. The girls made quick work of unbuckling themselves, and soon they were dropping their backpacks in the mudroom and racing into the kitchen. Only Noelle hung back as Trent finished hanging his coat on one of the hooks he'd recently installed along the wall.

"You look like you need a hug." He bent to pick her up. She nodded solemnly and wrapped her arms around his neck. "I'm sorry you had a rough day."

"I don't like it there." Her lips wobbled and tears filled her eyes. Then she placed her palms on his cheeks. "Your beard is soft."

"Yeah, it keeps me warm." He brushed her hair away from her face. "You want to grow one, too?"

"No, silly. I can't have a beard. Blankie keeps me warm."

"I know, sweetheart." Carrying her into the kitchen, he took a moment to get his bearings. Now that the girls were living with him, arriving home in the evening marked the start of his second shift. First shift was his actual job. Second involved mealtime and homework and baths before the girls went to bed. The overhead lights revealed scratched Formica countertops and original hardwood floors. Emma was poking through one of the lower cupboards where he kept canned goods.

"What are you looking for, Em?" He set Noelle on her feet.

"Tomato soup." She glanced back at him. "We're starving."

"How about spaghetti instead? I already have the sauce made. I just need to heat it up and boil the noodles."

Emma straightened, looked at Sadie, who stood on the other side of the U-shaped counter, then back at him. "Okay. We all like spaghetti. But Noelle doesn't want sauce. Just butter and cheese on hers."

"I like cheese." Noelle's shoulders reached her ears as she smiled and clasped her hands. "Lots and lots of cheese."

"You got it." Trent pushed up his sleeves and opened the cupboard where he kept his pots. He selected the largest one. "Why don't you all relax while I start supper?"

He put the pot in the sink and turned on the faucet. The girls had lined up on the other side of the counter and were staring at him. He pivoted with his back to them, set the pot on the stove and turned the burner to medium-high. Then he inhaled, counted to three and exhaled before facing them once more. "I take it this is about the babysitter?"

"Noelle's scared." Emma's chin tilted up. "She doesn't like it there. And we don't, either."

Trent thought back on his own childhood and the string of complacent babysitters he'd been stuck with after his father had died and his mom returned to work. He hadn't been happy with any of them, either.

"Okay." He nodded, trying to buy time to figure out what to do. "I think you all miss your dad and your routine in DC, and I don't blame you—"

"No." Emma shook her head. "This isn't about home. It's not about Washington, DC. We hate Mrs. Pine."

"*Hate*'s a strong word."

Emma frowned. "She's awful."

"If she spanked Sammy, she'll spank Noelle," Sadie said, her eyes wide. "If we're not there, we can't protect her."

"Why don't you tell me what happened?" He needed to get a handle on how serious this situation was. His gut told him it was serious. If everything they were saying was true, how could he send them back there?

"Sammy spilled his juice." Emma's hands clenched into fists at her sides. "Mrs. Pine didn't put it in a sippy cup. She handed him a glass filled to the top and told him to walk over to the table with it. He's so little. I tried to help him and she yelled at me. The juice sloshed and she got mad. Took away his juice, called him stupid and spanked him. But it was her fault. She shouldn't have done that."

While Emma spoke, the three girls had somehow joined hands. Their message was loud and clear. *Together we stand.*

Raking his fingers through his hair, he tried to come up with a solution. And came up blank.

One week. That's all the notice he'd gotten that he'd be raising the girls for the next year. One week in which Kevin had shipped bedroom furniture and their belongings here. Seven days for Trent to desperately attempt to shift his bachelor existence to the life of a single dad.

When Kevin and the girls had arrived, he and his brother had filled out paperwork at the elementary school and gotten them set up with a doctor and dentist here in town. They'd also gone to the bank where his brother had opened a generous joint account to pay for the girls' expenses.

On top of that, he'd set aside a large salary for Trent to hire a live-in nanny to take care of Noelle during the day and the other two outside of school hours. But in a small town like Jewel River, live-in nannies didn't exist. The only babysitter with any openings was Mrs. Pine, and after listening to Emma, Trent figured there was a reason few people trusted her to watch their children.

"I'll have a talk with Mrs. Pine." What else could he do? No one else was available.

"We aren't going back." Emma's eyes narrowed.

His temper stirred, but he threw a bucket of ice water on it. His nieces were settling into school and their new routine remarkably well. He didn't want to fight with them, not when he agreed with them.

"I don't know where else you can go." He opened his hands.

"The stables." Emma gave him a firm nod.

"Horsies!" Noelle had stars in her eyes.

"The stables aren't safe for you." He went over and dropped to one knee in front of them to get to eye level. "Your dad doesn't want any of you cold and hungry and in potential danger after school. And I don't, either."

"I'll be good, Uncle Trent, I promise." Noelle's face was so earnest, it tore at his heart.

"It's not about being good, sweetheart. It's about it not being the right environment for you." He took one look at the way their faces hardened and made a decision. "I hear you loud and clear. Don't worry. I'll figure out something. I'll talk to Mrs. Pine and make new arrangements."

But what those arrangements would be, he had no idea.

She'd never thought she'd call Jewel River home again. Yet here she was.

Gracie French tucked her legs under her body and carefully sipped her tea as she sat on her comfy, beige plush couch, a bargain she'd picked up from Goodwill last week, and stared at the snow swirling outside her living room window. She loved the view of R. Mayer Chocolates across the road with its pretty striped awning and decorated picture window. From her living room, she could watch everything happening on Center Street.

The movers Gracie had hired had unloaded everything Saturday afternoon, and her best friend, Brooke Dewitt, had helped her set up the apartment Sunday. For it only being Tuesday, she was reasonably happy with her progress unpacking. The small apartment above the dentist's office had been a blessing from the Lord. With two bedrooms, a galley kitchen, a small dining area and a large bathroom with a stackable washer and dryer, the price was right and the location perfect.

Now, if she could just find a job...

She couldn't take any old job, either. She needed one with benefits. One that would give her a future with health insurance, paid vacations and a retirement account. All the things she'd foolishly forfeited by listening to her dumb ex-boyfriend.

She sipped the tea again, savoring the orange flavor and spices, then reached over to drag a soft throw across her lap.

Gracie had been a fool for turning her back on her faith as a teen, partying too much, then quitting college and moving to Idaho to live with her boyfriend. She'd convinced herself he'd ask her to marry him and all would be right in her world. But five years later, the only ring she'd gotten was a phone call informing her he was moving out when the lease was up.

After months of tears, *why-me*s and plenty of conflicting advice from her coworkers, Gracie had finally faced facts. She'd made bad decisions, resulting in a pile of student loans and a low-paying job answering phones for a trucking company outside Twin Falls, Idaho. She'd promptly repented and asked God for help.

That had been almost two years ago. Her life had been getting on track. But Idaho had never felt like home, and she'd missed Brooke. So here she was. Taking a risk. Coming back to the town that had shaped her—for better and for worse—and trusting God would take care of her.

Lord, with Your help, I won't go back to the clingy girl I was. I'm relying on You and myself. That's it.

After another sip of tea, she set the mug on the end table and scrolled through her phone. For the past couple of days, she'd been waiting to hear from a recruiter. After three rounds of interviews, she was certain the work-from-home position was hers.

Her phone rang, making her jump. The recruiter! "Hello, this is Gracie."

"I'm afraid I have bad news…"

Her tongue stuck to the roof of her mouth as the recruiter explained the company had announced a hiring freeze yesterday afternoon.

This couldn't be happening. Not when she'd taken such a huge leap of faith to move here.

"I understand," she said. "If you hear of any other companies hiring, let me know." She ended the call and slumped into the couch. Tears pooled in her eyes, and she squeezed them shut, willing herself not to cry.

This was a setback. That was all. She'd find a job. The position didn't really matter, either, as long as it would help her get on track for the future.

She couldn't keep living paycheck to paycheck. As of last Friday, she was living no paycheck to no paycheck.

Gracie stood and tried to regroup. She gravitated to the window, her gaze locking on a tall cowboy striding to a pickup truck across the street. All she could see was his Stetson, Carhartt jacket, jeans and cowboy boots. As if sensing her staring at him, he paused and looked up. Straight into her window.

She almost clutched her chest as she realized who he was. Trent Lloyd. Looking finer than ever, and he'd always been attractive. Probably had a wife and four kids by now. He'd always been a good guy.

But she hadn't been a good girl.

With a quick step backward, she tried to will her pounding heart to slow down. What was he doing in town? She'd have to ask Brooke.

Would Trent remember her? If he did, would he still see the party girl she'd been?

Gracie padded to her bedroom. Over the past two years, she'd visited Brooke several times, and the people in Jewel River had been kind to her. They always asked how she was doing and wanted updates about her parents, who now lived in New Mexico. And she'd tell them what she knew, which wasn't much.

If anyone had a problem with her past, including Trent, she couldn't help it. All she could do was continue down the better path she'd chosen.

She shook off her nerves. Back to the online job boards. There had to be something out there for her—she'd keep searching until she found it.

Late Tuesday morning, Trent held Noelle's hand as they waited in line at Annie's Bakery. He'd dropped off Emma and Sadie at the elementary school, picked up several items from the feed store in town and made a quick stop at the accountant's office next to R. Mayer Chocolates. Noelle would not be going to Mrs. Pine's today. In fact, none of the girls would be in the woman's care ever again.

His blood still boiled at the phone conversation he'd had with the woman last night after the girls had gone to bed.

He'd done his best to keep an open mind and an even temper. He'd mentioned her spanking Sammy. She'd told him the kid needed a firm hand. Then he'd asked if she smoked in front of the children. Her defensive tone had quickly morphed to anger, and she'd claimed that the brats drove her to smoke. He'd politely told her he no longer needed her services.

As everyone in line shuffled ahead, he checked on Noelle. At his request, she'd left her blankie in the truck. Her big blue eyes took in the place. What did she think about all this? A new place to live. No dad around. A scary babysitter.

He'd let her down.

"Hey, Noelle, want a boost so you can see the doughnuts?" He held his arms out. She practically jumped into them, and he hiked her up on his hip. Why he felt such a fierce need to protect her, he couldn't say. She seemed so innocent, so tiny, so full of sparkly joy, that he wanted to keep her safe from every bit of pain life threw at her. Getting her away from Mrs. Pine was a step in the right direction.

"Can I get that one?" She craned her neck to the side and pointed around the man in front of them. Trent followed her finger. Pink icing and sprinkles. He wasn't surprised.

"You got it. Should we pick out some cookies for your sisters?"

"And for me, too." Her sweet voice made him chuckle.

"For you, too. We'll get a dozen. How does that sound?" She clapped her hands. "Yum!"

They reached the front of the line, and Anne Young, the bakery owner in her early sixties, beamed at him. "Howdy, Trent. This must be one of your beautiful nieces I've been hearing so much about. Hi, there, sunshine."

"I'm Noelle," she said proudly.

"Well, I have a doughnut with your name all over it." Anne bent to select one.

"You do? It says Noelle?"

Anne straightened, laughing. "No, but it's pink with sprinkles. What do you think?" She held up the exact one Noelle wanted.

"It's my doughnut, Uncle Trent!" Her mouth formed an O, and her eyes grew impossibly round. "She knew!"

"She sure did." He hitched his chin to Anne. "We'll take a dozen of your chocolate-chip cookies, three more of those doughnuts and two crullers."

As Anne boxed everything up, he realized she might be able to help him.

"Hey, Anne?"

"Yes?"

"I'm without a babysitter at the moment. You don't happen to know anyone who might be interested in watching Noelle during the day and the girls after school, do you?"

She thought about it a moment and shook her head. "I'm sorry, I can't think of anyone off the top of my head. Brooke has her hands full with the twins. Reagan's running her store and due to have the baby next month. Erica's the busiest woman I know and, from what I can tell, Gracie has a job lined up already."

"Gracie?" So, it had been her he'd seen in the window earlier. Gracie French. All grown up into a beautiful woman. He hadn't seen her since…the night he wished he could forget.

"Gracie French. She moved into the apartment above Roger's dental office. Brooke is tickled pink she finally returned."

Gracie was back. They were four years apart. As a senior in high school, it had bothered him to see the freshman hanging out with the party crowd. He personally didn't have anything against her, though.

Catching a glimpse of her earlier had stirred something inside him that he didn't like. Temptation. And temptation could distract him. He prided himself on the way he ran Moulten Stables, spending extra time going over accounts and checking the tiniest details of each horse's stall, feed, tack—you name it. Managing the high-end horse-boarding facility was a dream come true, and he was already struggling to give it maximum attention now that he had the girls. He didn't need another distraction.

"Here's what I'd do if I were you." Anne leaned across the counter. "Go to the Legacy Club meeting tomorrow night. You're sure to see Christy Moulten. She'll know of anyone who might want to babysit."

The Jewel River Legacy Club. He'd forgotten about it. Trent wasn't into meetings and clubs, so he'd never given it a thought when his buddies around town had mentioned it.

Even if he wanted to attend the meeting, he didn't see how he could. He had no one to watch the girls.

Anne rang him out and handed him a receipt. "I'd tell you to call Christy, but she's always busy at the nursing home, then off on an adventure with Angie. Go to the meeting." She handed him a bag with their goodies and waved goodbye to Noelle. "Oh, and Trent?"

"Yes?"

"Bring the girls to my place tomorrow. I'll watch them for you."

He smiled so big the corners of his mouth cracked. "Thanks, Anne. I will."

Looked like he was out of excuses. The Jewel River Legacy Club meeting might provide the solution he needed.

"Ready to see the horses?" he asked Noelle.

"Horsies!"

Chapter Two

After a night of troubled sleep and a morning of online searches yielding no job leads, Gracie put on her coat and headed down the staircase to the parking lot out back.

She needed chocolate.

About an inch of snow covered the ground. The frigid temperatures made her wrap her scarf more tightly around her neck, and she bustled through the alley and across the street to Reagan's shop. Inside, mellow jazz music and the rich aroma of chocolate greeted her.

She could live right here. Set up a cot and stay forever. Her idea of perfection.

"Gracie!" Reagan's baby bump preceded her as she held out her arms.

Gracie hugged her a beat too long. She'd gotten to know Reagan through Brooke, and she appreciated the calm, compassionate woman.

"I'm so glad you're here." Reagan stepped back. "How did the move go? Do you want a chocolate?"

"It went great. Everything's unpacked—for the most part—and I love my apartment. I have a terrific view of your pretty front window. The St. Patrick's Day theme couldn't be cuter. And, yes, I need chocolate."

Reagan laughed and returned to her spot behind the counter. "What will it be? Nuts? Caramels? Strawberry? Pretzel?"

All of the above? Gracie took off her coat. "Surprise me."

"Ooh, you're adventurous today."

"I guess you could say that. I'd call it more desperate than adventurous, though."

"Why? What's going on?"

"The job I was so sure of? It fell through. They announced a hiring freeze."

"Oh, no!" Her smile slid away in sympathy. "This calls for extra chocolates."

Another reason she liked Reagan—the woman got her.

"Do you know anyone around here who's hiring?" Gracie asked, eyeing the display case full of trays of elegant chocolates.

"Patrick Howard is going to need a receptionist for the service dog training center, but he doesn't think he'll be hiring until this summer."

"I can't wait that long."

"You might try the medical clinic. They always seem to need help with answering phones or billing."

"I could do that." Maybe there was hope.

"And get on the substitute teacher list." Reagan handed her a small box with an assortment of chocolates. "My treat."

"No, I'll pay—"

"I insist. Now, why don't you have a seat, and we'll catch up for a while?" Reagan led her to the one table in the joint. She'd put it there so her friends and family would have a place to sit and chat while she worked.

They brainstormed companies Gracie could contact and discussed Reagan's plan for when the baby arrived later next month. Then Gracie hugged her goodbye and hurried across the road to the parking lot where her car sat under a layer of snow. She started it up and scraped ice off the windows. When she buckled into the driver's seat, she shivered.

First stop? Brooke's house. Gracie needed to tell her about the job problem. After that, she'd head to the medical clinic and the elementary school. If she had to piece together an income until the right job came along, so be it.

At least she had supportive friends here. And she'd saved enough money to survive for three months without any income—if it came to that. She hoped it wouldn't come to that.

When the car was sufficiently warm, she drove to Brooke's. In the summer, she'd be able to walk to her friend's house. She embraced that thought. Although, with Brooke getting engaged to Dean McCaffrey last month, it was questionable how long Brooke would live there. The couple might want to buy a different house to start their new life together.

A few minutes later, Brooke ushered Gracie inside, and they settled into the living room with her identical twin daughters, who'd recently turned two. The girls showed Gracie their dolls.

"I love her cute outfit." Gracie smiled at Megan and cradled the doll. "What's her name again?"

"She Susie." Megan nodded solemnly.

"Here. Dis Ticky." Alice elbowed Megan out of the way to hand Gracie her doll. Megan gave her sister a scowl.

"Ticky?" Gracie made a production out of holding both dolls. "Ticky and Susie are darling. Just like you two."

Alice grinned and yanked the doll from her. Megan continued standing there with her hands clasped.

"I think Susie might need a bottle." She gently set the baby back in the girl's arms. Megan nodded, clutched the doll and ran off to join her sister in the corner with doll furniture, a play kitchen and a basket of toys.

"Do you like the apartment?" Brooke crossed one leg over the other. Her black curls fell down her shoulders, and her dark blue eyes watched Gracie carefully.

"I love the apartment. It's perfect. And the view is amazing. I can see Reagan's shop right from my couch. Although, now that I'm thinking about it, that could be a problem. I'll want chocolate all the time. She loaded me up with an assortment just now."

"I don't know how she does it, but they are positively the best chocolates I've ever eaten."

"I know. She has a gift," Gracie said. "So… I got some bad news this morning."

Brooke frowned. "What's going on?"

"The recruiter called. The company I was so sure of? They're on a hiring freeze. I'm back to square one."

Instead of looking concerned, Brooke's face broke into a smile. "This is great."

"Me being unemployed is great?"

"No, silly—" she waved the question away "—the timing. Mom just called and said Trent Lloyd needs a nanny."

Trent Lloyd? Gracie was pretty sure she went green at the mention of his name. She couldn't take care of his children. For one thing, even from the window two stories up, she found him terribly attractive. For another, she would never forget the last, and only, extended interaction she'd had with him. The final day of her freshman year. She'd gotten a ride with the Doone boys out to the old Platte bridge where everyone—okay, not everyone, just the popular kids—hung out on Saturday nights. After a while, she'd stumbled away, afraid she was going to be sick. But a strong arm had helped steady her.

Trent. Even now, she remembered the disappointment and concern in his eyes. She'd felt judged, and she'd been too immature and too inebriated to handle it. He'd told her it was time to sober up. She'd said a few choice words to him. His jaw had clenched, and she'd wondered if she'd gone too far.

At which point, he'd tossed her over his shoulder—who knew the tall senior could pack so much muscle on his frame?—and driven her home.

Home. The one place she'd never wanted to be back then.

Since that night, she hadn't seen Trent, but she'd thought about him plenty, mostly in shame.

Had it been wise to start drinking alcohol so young? No. She'd wanted to fit in. She'd been insecure. Over the past two years, she'd had a lot of time to think about her decisions, and she attributed some of them to an overall feeling of inadequacy. Didn't really matter now. She would make better choices in the future.

"I don't think Trent would be interested in me for the job." Gracie traced the hem of her sweater, keeping her eyes downcast. Brooke had never been allowed to go to the old Platte bridge, and Gracie hadn't told her about that night. She'd kept it inside. Where it belonged. Brooke knew all her other secrets, though.

"Why wouldn't he? You're amazing with kids, and you live close to his house. It would be ideal."

"I need a job with benefits. You know, health insurance? A retirement plan?" Her throat tightened saying the words. She *did* need benefits, but that wasn't the reason she was pushing back about the job.

"I know you do." Brooke lightly bit the bottom corner of her lip. "Maybe this could work in the meantime. He'll only have the girls for a year or so."

"Wait, Trent isn't married?" Why had she thought Brooke was talking about his own children?

"No. Those are his nieces. His brother's girls."

"Why don't I remember him having a brother?"

"When his mom remarried, his stepbrother, Kevin, was away at college. And then, after Trent graduated from high school, his mom and stepdad moved down south. She passed away a while back."

"Ah." It made sense. What didn't make sense was a gorgeous, caring man like Trent still being single. "What's he like now?"

"Still Trent. Extremely knowledgeable about horses. Upstanding citizen. Still pretty cute, if you ask me, but don't tell Dean I said so."

Gracie chuckled. "I won't."

"Yeah, it caught everyone off guard when his nieces arrived."

"Why is he raising them?" She mentally sorted the possibilities of why Trent's brother couldn't raise his own kids for a year. Prison sentence? Rock star on tour? Famous architect designing a building in Dubai?

"Trent's stingy on details, but apparently Kevin has a work commitment for the next year or so."

"Where does he work?"

Brooke shrugged. "As far as I know, he works for the government. But he might be in the armed forces."

"Huh." Government or military. Made sense. "How many kids are we talking about?"

"Three girls. Mom said the youngest, Noelle, is one of the cutest kids she's ever seen."

"Yeah, but your mom loves children."

"True, but she's extremely biased toward the twins. If she says the girl's cute, you know she is."

A nanny. Maybe it could work—if it was for anyone other than Trent.

They talked for another half hour. Then Gracie hugged her goodbye.

"I'm stopping at the clinic and school to put in applications." Gracie pulled on her gloves at the front door.

"Smart thinking." Brooke held the door open for her. "But you should seriously consider the nanny job."

"Maybe." She gave her a weak smile. Even if she thought about it all night, it wouldn't matter. Trent knew she'd been a mess as a teen, and if he had any idea about all the other mistakes she'd made, he wouldn't want her within twenty feet of his nieces.

She'd stick to her plan. Whatever that was.

He hoped this wouldn't end up being a waste of time. Trent nodded in greeting to Clem Buckley as he took a seat in the community center that evening. A lively crowd chatted in clusters near the tables shoved together to form a U. Cade Moulten, his boss, spotted him and came over with a grin.

"Hey, Trent, you finally changed your mind." Cade shook his hand.

"Just for tonight." There was no way he was making this a regular thing. He wasn't into activities that would take him away from the stables—or the girls—on a regular basis.

"Did you hire Elijah?" Cade asked.

"Yeah, he's excited about the job." They'd agreed to hire the eighteen-year-old high school senior to work at the stables in the evenings and on weekends alongside their other part-timer, Jim. Now that Trent had the girls, he needed extra help, and Elijah had proven himself trustworthy time and again as he'd volunteered with all the horses, not just his own. He was the only teen boarder who wasn't on the rodeo team, giving him more time to work. "With the spring rodeo season almost here, he'll be able to help the team load and unload their horses for practice in between his chores."

"Good. If either of you need time off, just holler. Ty and I will take care of the stables." Ty was Cade's brother, a quiet local rancher Trent had always gotten along with.

Erica Cambridge moved to her spot at the podium, and Cade returned to his seat. Trent mentally sighed in relief that Cade's mom, Christy, was sitting next to Cade. Good. He'd be able to talk to her after the meeting about potential babysitters.

"Welcome, everyone." In her early thirties, Erica might be all smiles, but she had a reputation for being no-nonsense. Trent had spent enough time around her and her husband, Dalton, to respect them both. "Clem, would you get us started?"

The tough former rancher used to intimidate Trent, but he'd learned to admire Clem. The man said exactly what was on his mind, was sharp as a tack and knew good horseflesh when he saw it. Clem stopped by the stables at least once a week to check out the horses.

Trent liked to think that's how it would have been if his own father had lived—with his dad stopping by the stables to discuss the horses and talk to him. A nice thought, but he had few memories of his father. He'd died when Trent was younger than Noelle.

After saying the Pledge of Allegiance and the Lord's Prayer, everyone sat down, and Erica brought up old business.

"The Easter egg hunt is next month," she said. "Since the weather is always atrocious, Dalton and I are offering to host it at the Winston." The Winston was a pole barn converted to an event center on her and Dalton's ranch.

"What's wrong with here?" Clem crossed his arms over his chest.

"A few people mentioned the space being a problem."

"It's too small." Christy turned to Clem. "And with the carpet recently replaced, no one wants mud tracked in here."

"Where are you going to hide eggs in that big pole barn?" Clem scoffed. "Are you just going to toss 'em on the floor and let the kids scramble for them? Sounds like a disaster waiting to happen."

Trent had worried the meeting would be boring, but this was actually entertaining.

"No, *Clem*, we aren't tossing the eggs on the floor." Christy's chin bobbed. "Erica is bringing in hay bales, and we'll put out a call to borrow potted plants and trees, too. We'll have plenty of spots to hide the eggs."

"Oh, Erica?" Angela Zane waved her hand.

"Yes, Angela?"

"Henry and I have an inflatable bounce house you can use. The little ones might like that."

"Great. We'll have to talk to someone about safety issues—"

"Already on it." Henry Zane, Angela's husband and the town's building inspector, shuffled the papers in his hands. "Ed and Dean said they have leftover rubber flooring they're willing to donate to put under it."

"Fantastic. Thank you." Erica nodded to Mary Corning, who was raising her hand. "Yes, Mary?"

"This would be the perfect time to install a few zip lines. Right inside the event center. Then the kiddos could swoop in and grab the eggs like superheroes."

Zip lines? Had Trent heard her correctly?

Erica winced. "Sorry, no can do. We don't have the permits for that."

"But if you can have a bounce house, I don't see why you can't have a few zip lines." As Mary, Henry and Erica argued about safety, Trent let his mind wander. The girls would like the Easter egg hunt. He planned on taking them, for sure. He wondered if they were doing okay with Anne. They'd been a little shy at first when he'd dropped them off at her house, but by the time he'd left, they'd been happily discussing brownies with her.

"We've been over the zip line thing, Mary." Clem shook his head in disgust. "Let it go. Jewel River doesn't need them. It's winter half the year here."

"That's why I thought having them indoors would be a smart solution." Mary was getting huffy.

"A solution to what?" Clem opened his hands as if confused. "There's no problem needing solved. Stick to your kettle corn—"

"Now wait just a minute—" Mary's face grew red.

"Stop." Erica held her arms out to each side. "Mary, Clem does bring up a good point. Do you think your crew would be able to provide kettle corn for the egg hunt?"

Trent doubted she'd be pacified by such an obvious ruse to change the subject.

Mary's face broke into a smile. "Of course, hon. Don't you worry. We'll have it ready."

Guess he was wrong.

"Moving on…" The meeting continued. Just as his hopes soared that it was over, the lights dimmed, and audiovisual equipment came out.

"We're in for a treat, everyone," Erica said. "Joey sent us a preview of his idea for this year's Shakespeare-in-the-Park movie, *Taming of the Shrew: Throw Her into Jewel River*."

Angela nodded proudly and looked around the tables. "Joey is going all out with this one."

Trent vaguely recalled that Joey was Angela's grandson. Still in high school, if he remembered correctly. Elijah had raved about his skills with digital special effects.

Everyone turned their attention to the screen. A few titters filled the air when Lars Denton appeared. Lars worked as a ranch hand on Winston Ranch for Erica and Dalton. A graphic zoomed over his cowboy hat, and a low male voice narrated.

"Petruchio needs a wife, but Katherina has other plans." Janey Denton, Lars's wife and local second grade teacher, appeared on the screen. She wagged her finger at him. The voice continued, "Can he tame her temper? Or will he have to toss her into Jewel River to cool it down?"

The women around the table all groaned.

The clip continued. "But Katherina won't go quietly." On horseback, Janey galloped past Lars and knocked off his cowboy hat. A few of the women let out a whoop. "A sassy cowgirl and a sudden tornado could change everything." A digital cyclone whirled across the screen, leaving rubble behind. "Be there. Or get thrown into the river, too."

There were so many things Trent wanted to ask. Why was anyone being tossed in a river? How did a sudden tornado fit into the original play? He was no expert on Shakespeare, but he doubted this movie was staying close to the script.

The meeting finally ended. Trent stood, shaking out each stiff leg. Then he crossed the room to where Christy was arguing with Clem about whether a slow roll at a stop sign counted as a stop. Trent knew better than to ask questions regarding her driving. She'd had her license revoked more times than anyone could count. He tapped on her shoulder.

"Oh, hi, Trent." In her midsixties, Christy had a blond bob and wore stylish clothes. "What's going on with you? How are the girls? I would love to bring Tulip over. I think they'd adore her."

"They're good. I'm sure they'd like the dog." Tulip was a regular visitor to the stables. Trent wouldn't admit it to anyone, but even he had a soft spot for the little Pomeranian trained to be a therapy dog. "Um, I have a question for you."

"Go ahead."

"Do you happen to know anyone who might be available to babysit the girls?"

"For a Friday night? So you can go on a date?" Her face glowed with hope, and he felt bad disappointing her. Dating was too complicated for him to consider. It led to love and marriage and kids. He could barely handle his current situation.

Horses made sense to him. Relationships were way over his head.

"No, no dates. I'm looking for a full-time nanny."

A look of confusion crossed her face. "Stella Pine didn't work out?"

"No."

"I can't say I'm surprised." She snapped her fingers. "I have the perfect person for the job."

He held his breath.

"Gracie French. She arrived in town a few days ago, and according to Brooke, her job fell through."

Gracie? He tried not to wince.

"Any other options?" He kept his tone polite.

She took a few moments to think it over. "Not really. I'm sorry, Trent. There are a bunch of us who are happy to help you out when we can, though, until you find someone." She patted his arm. "Talk to Gracie."

"It's important to have someone the girls feel comfortable with. Especially, Noelle." He had no idea what kind of life Gracie had been living, and he didn't want to find out. Besides, he'd always found her too pretty.

"Are you kidding me? They will love her. She's bright and bubbly and sweet as candy."

"I'll keep that in mind." He tipped his cowboy hat to her. "Thank you."

On his way back to Anne's, Trent weighed his options. He could at least talk to Gracie. Keeping Noelle at the stables today had only lasted a few hours before he'd had to take her home or risk her getting sick from the cold. She'd loved being out there, but her red nose and cheeks had concerned him. No, he needed a full-time nanny. Immediately.

If it meant he had to interview Gracie French, he'd reach out to her tomorrow. The girls were too important to him. They needed stability. But was Gracie someone who could give it to them? He'd try to find out.

Chapter Three

Her inbox showed eleven new emails. Gracie balanced her laptop on her knees. She'd woken a little after seven, showered, brewed a pot of coffee, read the Bible, written in her journal and prayed. Now she was ready for cup number two, but first, she said one more prayer. *God, please let there be a request for an interview in there.*

As she sat on the couch, she lifted her gaze to the window. Another overcast day. It looked brutally cold from her warm room. She drew her cardigan tighter around her body and clicked on the inbox.

Seven sales ads. Three newsletters—none of which she remembered signing up for—and a reminder from her dentist in Idaho that she was overdue for a cleaning.

Disappointment crashed down hard. Her fingers trembled as she reached for the mug of coffee next to her.

No big deal. Last night, she'd spent hours applying for eight positions she could do remotely, but none seemed like they'd be a good fit. Her local job search had been equally demoralizing. The medical clinic didn't need any help—not even part-time—at the moment, and the elementary school had referred her to their website to apply to be a sub. The mountain of online forms to fill out wouldn't bother her except the school receptionist flat-out said they had a full roster of substitute teachers.

The job hunt wasn't looking good.

Her phone rang, and she almost spilled her coffee. Not bothering to check the screen, she held it to her ear. "Hello?"

"Gracie? This is Trent Lloyd. We, uh, went to school together. Kind of. I wanted to discuss something with you." His deep voice held a touch of vulnerability and, if she wasn't mistaken, nervousness. For some reason, that made her feel better.

"I know who you are, Trent." Why did her voice sound so squeaky and high? "What's going on?" As if she didn't already know.

"I'm in charge of my three nieces for the next year, and my babysitting situation didn't work out. I heard you might be looking for a job, and I'm wondering if we could talk."

"Sure." Why had she agreed? She didn't want him scrutinizing her and wondering if she was as out of control now as she'd been back then. "What time?"

"Are you available this morning?"

"I am." She literally had nothing on her agenda for today and for every day following. It was an odd feeling, not having a job.

"I can come there, or you can stop by the stables."

"I'll drive to the stables." She had no issue with him seeing her apartment, but she preferred to go there. Less revealing. Plus, she loved horses. "Give me fifteen minutes."

"Okay. When you get here, enter the barn and take a right. My office is at the end of the aisle."

After saying goodbye, she scrambled to her feet. She needed to change and put on makeup and do her hair…

Fifteen minutes? What had she been thinking? She needed a full hour to get ready.

Get a grip. This wasn't a night out on the town. It was a simple meeting with a down-to-earth guy who needed a nanny. And he wasn't going to hire her anyhow. Why would he?

She hurried to her bedroom and changed into jeans. Then she brushed her hair and dusted powder over her face, added light blush, a swipe of mascara and pink lip gloss. Good enough.

Her worn cowboy boots fit her perfectly, and she smiled as she threw on her winter coat and walked out the door. Most of her friends in Idaho would have told her to dress up for the interview, but jeans, a long-sleeved T-shirt, cardigan and cowboy boots felt right.

Who cared what Trent thought of her? A babysitting job wasn't her first choice anyhow. She would hear him out, come home and hit the job boards again.

She'd moved to Jewel River because it was the only place that felt like home. She missed her bestie. Missed the small town. Maybe it hadn't been the smartest move to relocate before having a firm job offer, but she couldn't bear to start over somewhere else, even if there were more opportunities in larger towns.

Part of being proactive about her future meant living near the only family she'd ever really felt a part of—Brooke's. Anne, Brooke and her brother, Marc, had always welcomed her into their home. Her own parents had barely known where she was or what she was doing. She'd had all the material things a girl could want, and none of it had mattered.

All she'd really wanted was someone to care about her. To feel like she was important to someone.

Five minutes later, Gracie parked her car and, with her chin high, took in the grounds of Moulten Stables. What a gem tucked so close to town. The large wooden barn contrasted against the pale gray sky, and horses lifted their heads in a nearby pasture. She entered the barn and made her way past stalls to the office. The door was open, but she paused in the doorway and knocked.

Trent rose from behind the desk and waved her inside.

If anything, he'd gotten even more handsome over the years. She guessed his height to be around six-three or six-four. Muscles filled out every inch of his frame, and a faint smile hid behind his trimmed mustache and beard. The warm air in the office enveloped her. She took a seat at the desk. For a horse barn, the place was swanky.

"Thanks for meeting me." He sat again, allowing his fore-arms to rest on the top of the desk. "How have you been?"

Why did the question feel so loaded?

"Good." She nodded, maintaining eye contact. "And you?"

"Good." He averted his gaze. His Adam's apple bobbed as he swallowed. "Not great."

Her eyebrows arched in surprise. He was admitting life wasn't great? In high school, he'd seemed to be in complete control. He'd been well-liked, gotten good grades and worn an air of confidence. "I'm sorry to hear that."

"I'm in a bind." He lifted his eyes—brown with gold flecks—to meet hers. "I need help with my nieces. Full-time help. If I could find live-in help, I'd take it."

Full-time, she might consider. Live-in? No way.

"Emma's nine, Sadie's seven and Noelle's four. The older two are in school all day, but Noelle needs someone to watch her while I'm working."

Gracie hadn't spent a ton of time around children, but if she had a choice, she'd choose the age range he'd mentioned. While she liked babies, she'd never taken care of one for longer than a few hours.

"My brother is away for work for the next year, possibly longer, and the girls need someone they can rely on, someone dependable and a good role model…" His voice trailed off. "I'm going to be honest. I didn't want to call you, Gracie."

He sounded apologetic and firm at the same time. It didn't prevent the crack ripping down her heart.

"Then why did you?" She couldn't quite keep the snap out of her tone.

"It's a small town. I'm out of options."

"I'm your last resort." She nodded, unsure why the words were cutting her so deeply. It wasn't like any of this was new to her. "You're worried I'll bring a fifth of whiskey with me in the morning, pass out and light the house on fire."

He winced. "No, no. Nothing like that."

"You don't think I'll be a good influence." She lowered her voice without meaning to. "Because I was a mess when I was younger."

Trent was correct. This *was* a small town, and that meant, whether she liked it or not, she'd be running into him often for the foreseeable future. Not everyone needed or deserved an explanation about her past, but Trent? Maybe he did. She might as well lay it out now and get it over with.

"I haven't forgotten that night at old Platte bridge." She kept her gaze steady to watch his reaction. "I wish I could say I spent the rest of high school as a model citizen, but I didn't. I was very far from my faith then, and I remained that way until about two years ago."

He didn't add anything, didn't ask any questions.

"I partied through college and dropped out after my junior year because my boyfriend moved to Idaho. Real smart, I know. And instead of waiting for an engagement ring and marriage, I moved in with him. Another point in my favor. I lived with him for almost five years. Then he informed me that we were done when the lease was up."

Shame lowered her eyelids, and she almost couldn't bear to look at him, to see how he felt about her confession. But she did. And she didn't know what to make of his expression. He might not know what to make of it, either. She didn't detect condemnation. Disappointment, maybe.

She got it. She was disappointed in herself, too.

"What did you do after he broke up with you?" he asked.

"I moved in with some friends from work. Cried a lot. Bought a Bible and a blank journal. Got real with Jesus. I repented. And I slowly got my life together. So, if any of that scares you or is a red flag to end this interview—or whatever this is—let me know now because I'm not repeating it, I'm not apologizing for it, and I'm not sharing it with anyone else around town, either."

A thick silence filled the air. She hadn't told anyone besides Brooke all that. Anne knew, of course, and Marc and Reagan, because Gracie had given Brooke permission to tell them. They'd never judge her for her past. They accepted her as is, and she loved them for it.

But Trent…he wouldn't accept her as is. How could he? He barely knew her.

"I appreciate you telling me all that. Don't worry. I don't go around gossiping." He dry-coughed into his fist. "Why did you move back here? Was it for a boyfriend?"

Irritation tingled in her veins. She supposed she didn't blame him. He needed to know if she'd changed.

"No. No boyfriend, and I don't plan on having one anytime soon. I'm here for me. I got my life together, and I'm doing things God's way now. Frankly, He knows best."

"I didn't mean it like that." His cheeks flushed. "I just… never mind."

A sense of peace filled her. "It's okay. Ideally, I need a job that pays benefits. I'm planning for my future."

"I can't offer benefits."

She figured as much. Curiosity got the better of her,

though. Now that she'd told him her secrets, she wanted to know more about him.

"What have you been doing since high school?" she asked. "How do you spend your time?"

"Me?" He tugged at the collar of his shirt. "Why?"

"Because I imagine if I work for you, we'll be seeing each other on a daily basis, and I want to have a firm grasp on what I'm getting into."

"There's not much to tell."

"Good. It won't take you long." She leaned back in her chair, keeping her head high. She wasn't letting him get out of at least a brief summary of his adult life.

"I've pretty much been all about horses since I was a kid. Went to Auburn University. Got a degree in equine science. Moved to Lexington, Kentucky, to work for a thoroughbred farm. Last summer, I got the call from Cade about managing this place, and here I am."

"No wife? No kids? No girlfriend?" It seemed impossible. A handsome, rugged, model-citizen cowboy didn't come around often.

"No, no and no."

"Why not?"

"Guess there's not enough of me to go around. The horses get it all."

They got a lot then because she'd never forgotten him.

"I want to thank you," she said softly. "I appreciate you taking me home that night."

"You mean when I tossed you over my shoulder and dropped you off on your front porch?" His voice had a teasing, nervous lilt. "I don't know why I thought it was any of my business."

"Maybe that's why I appreciate it. I was never anyone's business. Not even my parents'."

He frowned at that.

"I remember what you told me, too," she said. He squirmed. "You said, 'Someday you're going to wake up and realize you're worth more than this.' You were right. I did. It just took me a lot of years to get there."

His face had passed the flushed stage and gone fire-red.

She took pity on him and changed the subject. "Now, what exactly does this job entail?"

Relief flashed in his eyes, and he began going over the schedule—what time he needed to be at the stables, when the girls came home from school and so on.

"I'd like for them to stay at my house as much as possible. It's big. Six bedrooms. A real rambling two-story. There's room for you if you—"

"No." She held out her palm to him. "I'd be willing to come to your house every day, but I'm living in my own apartment."

"It's probably for the best. Don't want people talking." He folded his hands together. "I can't offer you the job until you meet the girls. Not after what happened with their last babysitter."

"I'm glad, because I'm not even considering the job until I meet them. I'm warning you now, I'm probably going to have to pass. Like I said, I'm looking for full-time with benefits—paid vacation, 401K, everything."

"We can talk about pay after you meet the girls—if they approve of you."

"Do you approve of me?" She shouldn't have asked it. Shouldn't have opened herself up to his judgment. What did she care what Trent Lloyd thought of her?

She was God's child. Her sins were washed clean.

But she still cared.

"Yeah. I approve." He smiled.

She smiled right back. "You're just saying that because you need a babysitter."

"I don't *just say* anything." His shoulders lifted in a slight shrug. "I tell it like it is."

For some reason, that thought warmed her soul. She wanted the truth. Made life so much easier.

"When can I meet the girls?"

"Why don't you stop by my house around four? It's across the road from here. You can't miss it."

"Will do. If you're not busy now, why don't you give me a tour of the stables? I'd love to see what you've got here."

His wide grin brought a shimmer to his eyes. "I never pass up a chance to show off the stables. Come on. Let me show you around."

And just like that, Gracie could actually picture herself working for him. She could see him becoming a friend. More than a friend?

Nope. Not going to happen. Keep your heart under lock and key. You're not messing up again. Get your life together first. Then you can think about dating.

"Lead the way."

"What's she like?" Emma dipped a carrot stick into ranch dressing later that afternoon. Noelle had spent the day with Christy—Trent would forever be in her debt for offering to watch his niece today—and on the way home from school he'd explained to the three girls that Gracie was coming over for them to meet her. And now Emma wanted to know what she was like? Tough question.

Trent dug around in the deli compartment of the fridge until he found cheese cubes. He tossed the bag onto the counter and glanced at the three girls sitting on stools, munching on carrots, each watching him like a red-tailed hawk on a telephone post.

The Gracie he remembered was nothing like the one who'd shown up at the stables today. That Gracie had been young and impressionable and on the wrong path. This Gracie was mature and honest and beautiful. He'd had a hard time looking away from her pretty blue eyes. Her long, wheat-blond hair hadn't helped his concentration, either. And her outfit? He'd always been partial to a woman in jeans and cowboy boots rather than something frilly or formal.

A guy like him appreciated a country girl like her.

And he'd found himself enjoying her company even more while he'd given her the tour of the stables. She was easy to talk to—easy to be around. He hoped the girls liked her because having Gracie as a babysitter would take a lot of pressure off him.

Has she really changed, though? You barely know her.

"She's younger than Mrs. Pine," he said.

"Is she younger than you?" Noelle reached for the baggie of cheese.

"Yes."

"How much younger?" Emma asked.

"Um, four years."

"So that makes her twenty-eight." Sadie held out her palm to Noelle, who dropped cheese cubes into it one by one.

"I suppose it does."

"Is she mean?" Noelle asked.

"No. She's not mean." He leaned against the counter. "You can let me know what you think of her. If you don't like her, I'll figure out something, but it won't be staying with me at the stables."

"It's cold there." Noelle turned to her sisters and rubbed her forearms. "Brr...but I liked the horsies."

A knock on the front door sent his pulse flying.

"That must be her. I'll be right back." He held up his finger and made his way down the hall to open the front door. Gracie's lips curved into a smile that met her eyes. A soft, cream scarf was wound around her neck, and her blond hair floated over her shoulders down her back.

"You made it." Being so close to her almost knocked the wind out of him.

"Like you said, I couldn't miss it. Right across from the stables."

He ushered her inside and helped take off her coat. Then they went to the kitchen. The girls had moved from the counter to the table tucked into the nook. A curved wall of windows gave a nice view of the backyard, and maroon-and-tan-checked curtains framed them.

Lord, please let this meeting go well. Until this moment, he hadn't realized how much hope he'd had since talking to Gracie this morning.

"Girls, this is Gracie French." He nodded to the trio. "Gracie, this is Emma, Sadie and Noelle."

"It's a pleasure to meet you." Beaming, Gracie took a seat in the chair closest to Emma. "How do you like Jewel River so far?"

"It's really cold here, but I like my teacher." Emma's tone was noncommittal.

"I like this house," Sadie said quietly.

"I like Uncle Trent!" Noelle was sitting on her knees, and she rose up on them. "And the horsies, too." She pointed toward the hall, where the front porch faced the stables.

"I went over there this morning and saw the horses." Gracie talked to the girls like she would a friend, and Trent appreciated it. "They're beautiful, aren't they?"

With her eyes wide, Noelle nodded.

"You moved here a couple of weeks ago, right?" Her gaze went from girl to girl.

"Twelve days," Sadie said.

"Close enough, Sadie." Emma shot a glare at her sister.

"I grew up in Jewel River," Gracie said. "But I haven't lived here since I graduated from high school. I just moved back on Saturday."

"Five days," Sadie said.

"Is Jewel River the same as when you lived here?" Emma's eyes sparked with interest.

"Mostly." Gracie leaned in toward them. "But some things have changed. There used to be a restaurant called Delroy's Tacos. My friends and I stopped in there all the time for chips and queso."

"Where was it?" Emma seemed to be calculating where it could possibly have been located and coming up short.

"Do you know where Dippity Doo Ice Cream is?"

"Yes, but it's closed for the winter."

"That's where Delroy's used to be."

As Trent watched them interact, he felt the stirrings of relief. Maybe this would work out.

"Uncle Trent, did you eat chips and queso at Delroy's?" Emma asked.

"I did. I ate a lot of tacos there, too."

"I love tacos." Noelle clasped her hands and fluttered her eyelashes.

"I love them, too." Gracie scrunched her nose in a smile to her. "Why don't you each tell me about yourselves? Emma, would you like to start?"

"I love chocolate and I hate onions. Braeden Jones gets on my nerves at school, but I really like Sophia and Lindsey."

"What's Braeden's deal?" Gracie tilted her head.

"He thinks he's so smart, and he's always showing off at recess."

"Is he cute?" Gracie asked.

Trent frowned. Why would that be relevant?

Not making eye contact, Emma lifted one shoulder. "I suppose."

"Mmm-hmm. Okay, Sadie, what about you?"

Sadie let out a small sigh. "I like oatmeal cookies, but only if they don't have raisins. And spiders scare me."

"They scare me, too." Gracie cringed. "How is school going for you?"

Silence. A shrug.

Maybe Trent needed to look into that. Sadie was extremely intelligent, but she was also shy.

"Do you have a favorite subject?" Gracie asked.

He had to hand it to her. She knew how to handle the girls tactfully. He waited for Sadie to say math.

"I like reading. I wish I could read a book every day."

Another thing he hadn't known.

"We should go to the library," Gracie said. "Then you can check out a stack of books and read as many as you'd like."

"Really?" Sadie looked as animated as he'd ever seen her.

"Sure. I need to get a library card, too. We can all get one."

"Even me?" Noelle asked.

"Yes, you, too." She turned to Noelle. "Now, Ms. Noelle, tell me about what you like and don't like. Emma likes chocolate and hates onions. Sadie likes oatmeal cookies without raisins—because, really, who wants raisins in their cookies?— and she's scared of spiders. What about you?"

Noelle thought about it for a moment. "I love Daddy and doggies. I wish I could bring Tulip home to sleep right on my bed with me every night."

"Who's Tulip?"

"Mrs. Christy's puppy. She's fluffy and the nicest doggie you could ever have."

"That's right. Her Pomeranian. She *is* cute. Is there anything you don't like?"

"I don't like the dark, and I don't like Mrs. Pine." Her little voice wobbled at the end.

A pang of guilt pierced Trent. He hadn't realized how tough it had been for Noelle to go to Mrs. Pine's each day. What had he expected, though? Mrs. Pine had shown zero interest in the girls, unlike Gracie, who asked them about themselves and was paying attention to what they told her.

"Do you have a night-light?" Gracie asked.

Noelle shook her head. "Daddy forgot to pack it."

"I think we should order you one."

"Will you come tomorrow?" Noelle leaned her elbows on the table and rested her chin on her fists.

"I'm not sure. I'll have to talk to your uncle first."

Emma stood and motioned for the girls to join her. "Come on. Let's talk to Uncle Trent."

She led the way down the hallway with her sisters in line, and Trent followed them. When they reached the living room, the girls got into a huddle. Then they all nodded, straightened and turned to face him.

Emma took a deep breath. "We'll take her."

Gracie figured they were coming to a verdict on if they wanted her as a babysitter or not. At the table, she stared out at the barren backyard.

If Trent offered her the job, she was accepting it. These girls had each other, yes, but the three of them wore their hearts on their sleeves, and she wanted to support them. She wanted to hear about their days and hash out Braeden's actions with Emma, read a stack of books with Sadie and chase away the darkness that Noelle feared.

Sure, the job wouldn't have benefits. It probably wouldn't

pay well, either. She could stretch her budget. Her apartment was cheap, her car was paid off, and besides her living expenses and student loans, she didn't need much.

The only uncertain element was Trent. Would he trust her with his nieces' care? Would a part of him wonder if she'd be a bad influence on them?

The four of them returned. Hmm. That was quick.

"Gracie, can I talk to you for a minute?" Trent cocked his head to the side.

"Sure." She got to her feet and smiled at the girls. Then she went with Trent to the front of the house, where he gestured for her to take a seat on the couch in the living room.

"The girls want you to be their babysitter." He sat on a chair opposite her. His knee bounced rapidly.

Her heart soared. They wanted her!

"I want to be their babysitter," she said firmly.

"But you don't even know the pay."

"I'll make it work somehow."

His face said it all—he hadn't expected her to accept the job. She probably shouldn't have taken it without knowing what it paid. If he offered anything above twelve dollars an hour, she'd be able to survive. If not, she might have to get a part-time job, too.

"I know having a job with benefits is important to you, and I can't offer you that. But I can offer you a generous salary. My brother has an account all set up to pay you. The girls are his world, and he can afford it. It's what he paid the sitter in DC."

Please be over twelve dollars an hour.

"It's twenty-five dollars an hour. There will be times I'll need you to work over forty hours, and I'll pay you overtime."

Twenty-five dollars an hour? She felt the blood drain from her face. She'd heard him wrong. There was no way he—or his brother—would pay that much for babysitting.

She'd never made that much in her life.

"I'm asking you to commit for a full year with the possibility of eighteen months." Trent's brown eyes were pools of sincerity. "I don't want to be in this position again. The girls need stability."

A full year. If she was careful with her money, she could pay down her student loans. And then...eventually, she could buy a house. In town.

As excitement built, she took a deep breath. She was getting ahead of herself. This job was for a year. She'd still have to find a new job after that.

Who cared? She'd landed in a win-win situation. Babysitting the girls *and* making good money.

Thank You, God!

"What do you say?" he asked.

"I say yes. I'm willing to commit to the year, possibly longer."

"If anything comes up that would be a negative influence on the girls, I'm reserving the right to terminate our arrangement on the spot."

"Understood." It didn't feel great having him question her integrity, but she didn't blame him. Not really.

"When can you start?" he asked.

"How about tomorrow?"

He grinned. "I was hoping you'd say that."

This is what happens when you trust God, Gracie. Sometimes you get more than you ever thought possible.

But she had to remember this *was* a job. Not a relationship. Nothing permanent. She was one hundred percent positive she was going to fall hard for the girls. As long as she didn't fall hard for their uncle, too, she'd be all right. At least, she hoped so.

Chapter Four

The following afternoon, Trent leaned back in his office chair at the stables and tried to calm his nerves. He'd been on edge since finding out the girls were coming to live with him. Would he be this keyed up the entire time they were here? Or was this just the figuring-it-out phase?

Last night, his nieces had chattered away happily after Gracie left. He'd had a good feeling about hiring her. She'd agreed to pick up the girls from school every day, and he'd explained appropriate snacks and the rules regarding homework. She'd brought up a number of other subjects he hadn't really thought about, like how much time they were allowed to spend on the iPad and if they had chores.

Logically, he knew he could rest easy with them in her care. But his mind kept coming to bad conclusions.

Had she changed? Or did she believe she'd changed but really hadn't?

He straightened and frowned. Who else could he have hired? He had no other options. And he wanted to trust her. But trust, for him, came hard. Probably due to losing his dad as a kid and not spending as much time with his mom as he would have liked since she'd had to work so much.

Busying himself with the daily hot list, he checked off the tasks he'd finished already. When Elijah showed up, he'd have him take care of the afternoon chores for the premier horses Moulten Stables boarded all winter. They affectionately called them the A-Team. Since the companies that owned those horses provided horseback riding with their expensive summer rentals, Moulten Stables was solely responsible for their care. Locals boarded their horses at the stables, too, but most of them took care of their animals on their own. Trent checked every horse throughout the day and also managed the day-to-day operations.

He loved his job.

"Checking in, Mr. Lloyd." Elijah appeared in the doorway. His face was ruddy either from the cold or from rushing over after school, and he wore clothing identical to Trent's: jeans, boots, a winter coat, stocking cap and gloves. "Is it okay for me to ride Scout before I work through my list? Tori's coming by, and she's riding Samantha's horse."

"That's fine. Take advantage of the daylight." Trent gave the kid a smile. "Am I going to get to meet this Tori? By the way, here's your list." He held out the paper and Elijah took it from him. He'd been raving about Tori for the past week. Seemed they were boyfriend and girlfriend or whatever the teens called it these days. Trent had never been able to keep up with trends.

"You want to meet her?" His eyes lit with excitement. "I'll bring her in as soon as she gets here."

"Let me verify that Samantha gave her permission to ride." Trent bent to open the bottom desk drawer where he kept hanging files. He thumbed through the tabs until he found the one marked "Fowlers," containing three folders. One for Matt, one for Lisa and one for their daughter, Samantha. The standard permissions he had each client fill out listed Victoria Klein. Good. The stables had become the place for the local teens on the high school rodeo team to hang out, and although they could be loud, they respected the horses and the facility. Trent liked the energy they brought. "You're good to go." "Okay, thanks. I'm going to watch for Tori." Elijah jogged away with the checklist clutched in his hand.

He guessed he'd better stay put until Elijah brought Tori back here to meet him. He had his own list of items to check off over the next couple of weeks, and he wanted to tackle a few of them before quitting time today. He'd been so busy on the home front, he hadn't been able to work on the extras, and it bothered him.

He'd give the tack room a thorough cleaning. It was tidy, but cobwebs and dust accumulated constantly. The facility had two tack rooms. One for the local boarders and one used exclusively for the A-Team. Only Cade, Trent, Jim and Elijah had access to that one. They each had master keys to unlock the facilities, the tack room and the horse stalls, too.

His thoughts drifted across the road to Gracie and the girls. What if Noelle was miserable with her? What if Gracie had forgotten to pick up Emma and Sadie? What if she'd gotten a wild idea in her head and taken off with his nieces? Put them in danger?

Where had that thought come from?

"Hey, Mr. Lloyd, this is Tori." Elijah stood next to a pretty brunette several inches shorter than he was. Her head seemed to shrink into her neck, but she stepped forward when Trent stood and thrust out his hand.

"Nice to meet you," Trent said.

The girl seemed petrified of him.

"I take it you ride?" he asked.

She nodded, not making eye contact.

"Are you on the rodeo team?"

She shook her head, clearly uncomfortable. He took pity on her. He understood being shy around new people.

"I won't keep you. Have fun out there," Trent said. "Elijah will take good care of you."

"Thanks, Mr. Lloyd." Elijah's face shined with teen adoration as he and Tori turned to leave.

Trent should go straight to the tack room, but he'd feel better if he knew the girls were okay. After the Mrs. Pine debacle, he owed it to them to have a good nanny. He got up and hurried to the doorway. "Hey, Elijah, I'm going to run home. Will you be okay here on your own? I'll only be gone a few minutes."

"Sure thing. I'll text you if anything comes up."

"Thanks." Trent locked his office. He wished he could have kept the good feeling about hiring Gracie, but all of the things she'd admitted from her past continued to land in his gut like hard pellets.

She'd been honest. Maybe too honest. No, he'd needed that transparency. In fact, he'd chalked it up in her favor. But now?

Maybe she wasn't partying, drinking or dating the wrong guy, but that didn't mean she was a good babysitter for the girls.

Yanking his keys from his pocket, he strode out the door to his truck. Didn't bother letting it warm up, just backed out of the spot and drove across the road to his house.

Why am I doing this? I should be giving her the benefit of the doubt.

The pastor's sermon from last week came to mind. He'd preached about putting the best construction on people instead of the worst. Trent ignored it. This wasn't about him—it was about his nieces' safety.

Gracie's car wasn't there. Uneasiness gripped him. As

he opened the back door, he listened for the girls or Gracie. Nothing. No one was home.

School had let out forty-five minutes ago. His house was only five minutes away from the school.

Don't panic. There's a reasonable explanation.

He didn't like this. Didn't like the fact that he had no idea where she was.

Had she taken Noelle somewhere and forgotten about the other two? What did he really know about her? Only what she'd told him. She should be here at home, fixing snacks for the girls and helping them with homework.

Trent clenched his hands into fists. He needed to get back for Elijah. He took out his cell phone and texted Gracie.

Where are you?

One strike against her—and on the first day. There had better not be another strike tomorrow.

If this didn't work out, what would he do?

Trent checked his phone, but she hadn't replied. Outside, he went back to his truck. Should he call the school? Drive around to look for her?

No. He'd give it half an hour. If he didn't hear from her by then, he'd start making calls. Either way, Gracie had some explaining to do.

"All right, ladies, let's get inside and have some snacks." Gracie parked in the driveway and opened the back door of her car for Sadie to get out. Then she lifted Noelle and set her on the ground. Emma had exited on the other side, and they all grabbed their backpacks and tumbled into the house.

"I can't wait to read this one." Sadie dropped her backpack in the mudroom and clutched one of her new library books to her chest. "And there's a whole series!"

"I know." Gracie widened her eyes, grinning. "I hope you love it. Then you can read them all."

Sadie backtracked to Gracie and threw her arms around her. "Thank you for taking us to the library. I have my own card!"

She stroked the girl's hair as she hugged her back. "You're welcome. We'll go every week."

"Really?" Her dark blue eyes shimmered.

"Yes, really." Gracie chuckled. "I love the library. I can get a stack of magazines, a new novel, cookbooks—anything I want. And it doesn't break my budget."

"I'm starving," Emma announced after hanging up her coat. She lugged her backpack into the kitchen. "I'm changing into my comfy clothes and getting out the snacks."

"Noelle and I made deviled eggs earlier. Plus, I cut up some raw veggies."

"Okay." She disappeared.

"Are you happy with your books?" Gracie asked Noelle. She held five picture books in her hands, and her baby blues gleamed with happiness.

"Can we read one now? The puppy one?"

"Let me see what kind of homework Sadie and Emma have first. Then we'll read it."

Her face fell, but she nodded and hurried through the kitchen. Her footsteps could be heard up the staircase, following her sisters. Only then did Gracie get out her phone to check her messages. The one from Trent made her heart race—in a bad way.

Where are you?

The three words felt like a big finger pointing at her, accusing her of a crime. She quickly typed a reply.

We went to the library. Home now.

As if on cue, the sound of his truck parking made her tense. The mudroom door opened, and Trent, with a menacing expression, slammed inside. The muscle in his cheek flickered.

"Where have you been?" he asked in a low voice.

"The library. Why?"

"You should have told me."

"I should have?" She was missing something, wasn't she?

"Yes. I stopped by ten minutes ago and you weren't here. None of you were here."

"Right, because we stopped by the library after school to get library cards and books."

"I didn't know that." By the way his neck was turning red, she could only assume his anger or annoyance or whatever he was experiencing was getting worse.

"Was I not supposed to get them library cards?" She tried to keep her tone neutral and light.

"I have no problem with library cards. I do have an issue with you not telling me where you are."

"Okay. Do I need to tell you everywhere I go?" If she did, it would put a serious damper on how she conducted her life, but if he insisted, she'd oblige. She'd always been more spur-of-the-moment than scheduled.

He didn't say anything. Just stared at her in that disapproving way. The longer he stared, the more she began to question herself.

Had she made a mistake by taking the girls to the library? It had seemed like an innocent side trip at the time. And it was only a few minutes from the house. Did Trent think she was irresponsible?

As the familiar insecurities trickled down, she recognized

them and lifted her chin. *I wasn't irresponsible. I had good intentions. I'm not beating myself up over this.*

The arguments she'd gotten into with her ex-boyfriend roared back. Always over a misunderstanding. She'd bristle and get defensive. He'd act like she was stupid. And before she'd known it, they'd be shouting. Then she'd apologize, scared he was going to leave her. Terrified her house of cards was about to flutter to the ground.

She wasn't going down that road. Better to diffuse the situation now.

Gracie looked through the doorway to make sure the girls were still upstairs. "Would you feel better if I texted you when we're going somewhere?"

The tension seemed to drain from him. At least a little bit. Then he nodded.

"You could have called me," she said as gently as possible. "I would have answered, you know. I never check texts when I'm driving, but I have Bluetooth for calls."

The girls came back downstairs, and their voices grew louder as they opened the fridge and took out the snacks.

"Uncle Trent! I want a puppy!" Noelle rushed into his arms. He picked her up and gave her a kiss on the cheek. "Are you home for good?"

"No, sweetheart. I have some more work to do." He set her back on her feet. "You be good for Gracie, okay?"

"I love Gracie." Noelle came over and wrapped her arms around Gracie's leg, then stared up at her with adoration.

Gracie's heart melted like the center of a grilled-cheese sandwich.

"And I love you, too." She gave her a hug. Noelle bounced away for snacks, leaving her alone with Trent. "I'd better supervise snack time."

"I'll, uh, be back in a few hours." He turned abruptly and walked out the door.

That entire interaction had been weird.

God, I know You brought me back to town for a reason, and I trust that You wanted me to watch over these precious girls. But their uncle? I don't know what his deal is. He's Your problem. I'm not tying myself into knots. I can't read his mind, and I don't want to.

And with that, she joined the girls as they plated up a variety of snacks. She'd take care of his nieces. Enjoy her time with them. And leave Trent and his bad mood alone.

"I'm scared, Uncle Trent." Noelle, clutching her pink blankie, tiptoed into the living room around ten that night.

It had been a long day, and he'd beaten himself up a few times for treating Gracie like she was a convicted felon on parole. In the moment, he'd been furious and scared. But as soon as he'd driven away, he'd felt guilty and foolish. Gracie was right. All he'd had to do was call her.

Why had he jumped to the worst conclusions?

"What's got you scared?" He patted his lap for her to climb up. He'd been watching a movie on television he'd seen a dozen times. Couldn't say he'd been paying attention to it.

"It's dark. I can't see anything when it's black out. I miss Daddy." Her voice caught at the end.

"I don't blame you for missing him." He helped her onto his lap, and she snuggled against his chest. "The dark won't hurt you, though. I'm here."

"You're big and strong."

"That's right."

"But what if a monster gets me when you're downstairs and you don't know it's in my room?"

"Nothing'll get past me." His cell phone rang. He checked the caller. Cade. "Sit tight. I'll be back in a jiffy, okay?"

With her lower lip jutted out, she nodded. He stood, shifting her to his spot on the couch, and answered the phone. "What's going on?"

"Are you at the stables?" Cade asked.

"No, I'm at home. Why?"

"I was driving by, and I saw lights on inside."

Trent instantly went into fix-it mode. "I'll go over right now." Then he remembered the girls. "Wait. I can't. I don't have anyone to watch my nieces."

"I'll turn around and check. Don't worry about it. Probably got left on by accident."

Trent didn't like the fact that his boss had to check on the stables instead of him. He didn't like a lot of things in his life at the moment. Mainly himself. "Thanks, man. Call me if you see anything out of the norm."

The call ended, and he mentally reviewed what might have happened. Before the girls were living with him, every night Trent would return to the stables ahead of closing time for a final walk-through. He no longer had that luxury and had to trust that Jim and Elijah were handling everything properly.

Were they handling everything properly?

His nerve endings tingled. He longed to throw on his boots and drive over there, but a glance back at Noelle with her blankie pulled up to her chin and her eyes wide with fright reminded him he had young ones to consider.

The stack of books Gracie had helped Noelle check out were sitting on the coffee table. He grabbed the top one and sat next to Noelle.

"How about we read a book, and then you can go back to bed? I'll check your room to make sure it's clear."

"I don't want to go back to bed. It's scary."

"I know. But you'll feel better after the book."

He opened the first page and began reading about two children making a gingerbread house. By the time he'd finished, Noelle had fallen asleep. He gathered her gently into his arms and carried her upstairs. After tucking her into her bed, he kissed her forehead and went back to the living room.

Cade had texted him.

The locals' section lights were left on. I switched them off and locked up.

Trent texted him a thank you and stretched out his body on the couch.

He prided himself on running a tight ship at Moulten Stables. He didn't like having to rely on other people, and he really didn't like when things weren't done correctly.

He'd have to keep a closer eye on the stables. And he might have to cut Gracie some slack. He wasn't sure he was capable of either, but he'd try.

Chapter Five

For three weeks, Gracie had been keeping things polite and professional with Trent. Whenever she took Noelle on an outing—visiting Christy to see Tulip was Noelle's favorite—she made sure she told Trent in advance. Every Tuesday after school, she took the girls to the library, and on the few occasions they'd gone to the store, she'd texted him beforehand. He wasn't as growly as he'd been when she'd first started, and for that she was grateful. But the easy way they'd talked to each other in the stables the day he'd hired her was nowhere to be found.

Did he only view her as an employee? She preferred to think of him as a friend, too.

What she had to discuss with him would be way easier if they were friends. As things stood now, she couldn't imagine the conversation helping her cause.

He'd be home soon. Gracie sat at Trent's kitchen table with the girls. She'd already overseen Emma's homework. Sadie didn't have any and was reading her book. Noelle was coloring her "homework."

Every weekend, Gracie printed out activity sheets for Noelle to work on throughout the week while her sisters did their homework. The four-year-old loved feeling like a big kid. She happily solved mazes, colored alphabet sheets and practiced cutting out shapes with her safety scissors.

"I have to do a book report." Emma shoved a folder into her backpack. She didn't seem her confident self today. "It's in May."

"What book are you reading?" Gracie asked, glancing at Sadie, whose face hid behind *The Lion, the Witch and the Wardrobe.*

"I don't know yet. It's an oral report." Her cheeks were pink, and she kept twirling a lock of hair that hung over her shoulder. Emma wasn't usually fidgety, so Gracie was surprised to see the girl flustered.

"Does getting up in front of the class bother you?" Gracie asked.

"No." She shook her head firmly. "I like talking to the class."

"Then what's the problem?"

Her little shoulders lifted in a shrug. Sometimes Gracie forgot how small and young the girl was. With her take-charge personality, she seemed older than her nine years.

"What if everyone makes fun of my book?"

"Why would they do that?"

"Sophia told Luke what she was reading, and some of the boys laughed at her during recess."

Gracie's memories of her school days rushed back. She remembered the angst of those years. Wanting to fit in. Trying desperately to avoid any situation where she might be humiliated. The insecurities had gotten worse in high school.

Maybe she shouldn't have tried so hard to fit in. It certainly hadn't gotten her far.

"No one likes being laughed at." Gracie debated how to handle this. "When I was your age, I probably would have found a book that most of my classmates liked, that way no one would make fun of me."

Emma's face brightened. "That's what I was thinking."

"And it's okay if you want to do that. But I hope you'll take a chance and choose the book you *want* to read. If someone makes fun of you for it, just tell them you loved it and to read it themselves. I'm guessing they'll back off."

She let out a long sigh. "Wouldn't it be easier to pick a different book?"

"Yes, it would be," Gracie said. "I know from experience, though, that once you start making decisions based on what you think everyone else likes, you lose touch with what *you* like. I wasted too much time worrying about what other people thought of me, and I wish I hadn't."

"You?" Emma's stunned tone made her smile.

"Yes, me."

"Yeah, Emma. Pick the book you want." Sadie set her book down. "If someone makes fun of it, you'll just tell them why they're wrong. You always stand up for yourself. I like that about you."

Emma sat up a little taller. Gracie wanted to hug Sadie for being so supportive.

"I liked the crocodile book you read to me, Em." Noelle looked up from the picture she was coloring. "You pick good books."

"See?" Gracie smiled. "We all agree. You have good taste. No need to worry."

"I think I'll read *The Phantom Tollbooth* for my oral report. My friend Jacie from back home got it for Christmas and said it was the weirdest book she'd ever read. She loved it."

"Well, there you go." Gracie nodded. "Great choice."

"I want to read it when you're finished." Sadie picked up her book again.

"Does the library have it? Or do I need to order you a copy?" Gracie swiped her phone and added it to her online order list. She'd been jotting down things she wanted to get the girls, like Play-Doh for Noelle, a pretty journal for Sadie, a jewelry-making kit for Emma and a few board games they all could play.

"If it's as good as Jacie says, I want my own copy." Emma snapped right back to her confident self. She turned to Sadie. "You can borrow it when I'm done."

"Thanks."

The side door to the mudroom opened with a creak. Trent had arrived. Noelle abandoned her crayons and raced to greet him.

"Uncle Trent, you're home! I want a puppy!"

Trent emerged into the kitchen carrying Noelle on his hip. "A puppy? Didn't you say that yesterday?"

"And the day before," Sadie said, not looking up from her book.

"Every day," Emma said crisply. "She says it every day."

"Ladies, why don't you go to the other room for a minute?" Gracie asked. "I need to talk to your uncle."

"About what?" Emma asked.

"Personal stuff."

Emma raised her eyebrows, but she and Sadie pushed back their chairs, and Trent lowered Noelle to her feet. As soon as the trio was out of earshot, Gracie motioned for him to join her at the table.

"What's going on?" He sat across from her.

"How do you feel about getting a dog?"

"I like dogs." He blinked, frowning. "But I don't know. I've never thought about getting one. Why?"

"Moving here has been hard on the girls, even though they're adjusting well. It's tough on them not having regular contact with their dad. A dog might help."

"You think so?" He seemed to be considering it. She relaxed.

"You have this big house and yard. Noelle is obsessed with Tulip. The other two love dogs, too."

"Noelle does have puppies on her mind." His playful smile sent a surge of hope through her. This was the man she'd toured the stables with, the one she could easily see being her friend.

"I'm kind of surprised you don't have one already. Are you allergic?" She was genuinely curious. From everything she'd seen of Trent over the past weeks, he was a guy's guy. Loved horses, spent the bulk of his day outdoors, seemed perfectly content as a bachelor.

"I'm not allergic." He rubbed his beard. "Would the dog stay with me when Kevin comes back to take the girls?"

"It depends. Do you want a dog forever? If you don't, this might not be a good idea. It wouldn't be fair to expect your brother to add a dog to his life without his permission."

"If it was a small dog, he probably wouldn't mind. Big ones bring in dirt and need long walks. I can't picture him having the time for that."

"Could you get a hold of him to find out?"

"I don't think I need to. If Kevin doesn't want it, I'll keep it when they leave." He stared out the windows. "It could be an Easter surprise for the girls."

"That might be pushing it. Easter is only a week and a half away." The holiday fell in late April this year.

"Yeah, you're right." He lightly tapped his fingertips on the table. "I'll talk to Patrick Howard before I do anything. Find out what dogs are best suited for the girls at their age. I'd need to train it. Buy supplies."

He had an openness about him today, and she figured she might as well take advantage of it. "While I have you here, I wanted to make sure you're okay with some of the things I'm ordering for the girls."

"What kinds of things?"

She found the note on her phone and read off each item. "Oh, and I'm adding a book for Emma's book report."

"I'm glad you brought this up." He angled his head to the side. "I got you a prepaid credit card for expenses that are sure to crop up for the girls. I don't want you paying for ice creams and supplies out of your own pocket, and this is easier than dealing with cash. I'll load more money on it as needed."

"You already pay me so much. I don't mind—"

"Kevin pays for it, and he wants the girls to have the things they need. If they need clothes or anything, just pay for it with the card. But let me know if you're buying anything over a hundred dollars."

"Of course. I'll get permission for any large purchases. And don't worry, I'm not going on a spending spree with it or anything."

"I know you aren't." His steady gaze made her freeze.

Was that a compliment? His tone made it feel more like a threat.

"Um, thanks." She still had the impression she was being scrutinized. Sure, she'd passed some of his tests—what they were, she had no idea—but she hadn't passed them all. At least, that's what he seemed to be implying. Maybe she was reading things into it that she shouldn't.

"It's upstairs. I'll leave it on the counter tonight—unless you need it now."

"I don't need it now." She pushed herself to stand. "Thanks for listening."

"A dog is a good idea." He smiled—and she wasn't prepared for it. He didn't smile all that often. It brightened his face, made him look younger. "Next year if Kevin doesn't want to keep the mutt, it can come with me to the stables every day."

"You could always get two dogs—one for you and one for the girls." She made her way to the mudroom to get her coat, boots and purse.

"One's plenty." He followed her. "I'm taking the girls to the Easter egg hunt on Saturday. Want to join us?"

Her pulse leapt to life. Did he have any idea how lonely the weeknights and weekends had been? She typically had coffee with Brooke on Saturday morning, and then there was church on Sunday, but she'd been struggling with what to do with the rest of her time off. "Sure."

"Don't feel obligated. I know you probably need a break from the girls, so I—"

"No, no. I don't need a break. I like being with them. I want to go with you guys."

"Okay, should I pick you up, or do you want to meet us there? They're having it at the Winston."

"Pick me up." She shoved her right foot into her boot.

"What time?"

"What time does it start?" She yanked her left boot on.

"Um, I have to check. I think it's at eleven in the morning. I'll get back to you when I know for sure."

"Okay. I'm going to say goodbye to the girls quick." After striding through the kitchen, she stopped at the bottom of the staircase. "Emma, Sadie, Noelle?"

Footsteps thundered down, and the girls stood before her.

"I'm leaving. I'll see you tomorrow." She hugged them, and kissed each girl on the top of the head. "Noelle, don't forget to plug in your night-light, okay?"

"Okay!" Noelle hugged her again. "Why don't you stay here? You can sleep in my bed."

Gracie's heart squeezed. "Remember what we talked about?" She crouched to Noelle's level and brushed the girl's hair behind her ear.

"I can tell Jesus when I'm scared. He's always here." Her lower lip plumped. "But I can't see Him."

"You can't see the wind, either, but that doesn't mean it isn't there. You pray and ask God to protect you. He won't let you down."

Noelle gave her one more big hug. Then Gracie straightened, waved and went to the mudroom with Trent behind her.

"Thanks for that," he said, opening the door. Cold air blew around her. She couldn't wait for summer to arrive.

"For what?"

"For giving Noelle good advice. For telling her to pray."

"Of course." She gave him a big smile. "See you tomorrow."

"Yeah. Be careful."

"I will." And with that, she left. Trent confused her. Most days he'd give her a gruff *How'd it go?* And she'd fill him in then leave. But today? He'd listened. Seemed to appreciate her. For the most part.

Progress. She'd take it.

After Jim arrived the following afternoon, Trent drove to the warehouse where Patrick Howard had recently opened a service dog training facility. Next door, Jewel River Veterinary Service, owned by his daughter, Mackenzie—Cade's wife—had several vehicles in the adjoining lot. He parked, then took long strides to the entrance. Inside, he scanned the large open area for Patrick.

Hard to believe he was considering getting a dog. As soon as Gracie had mentioned it yesterday, he'd thought, *Yep, good idea.* In fact, he wasn't sure why he'd never gotten one. He'd always loved dogs.

Tall, fit and in his early sixties, Patrick stood in a large enclosure with three dogs. Two appeared to be Labradors and one was a German shepherd. Patrick spotted him and waved him over.

They shook hands, and Patrick had his assistant take over for him.

"What brings you here?" Patrick asked.

"I need some advice."

"I'm all ears."

"I'm considering getting a dog. I'm looking for a breed that will be good for the girls, but after they return home with their dad, the dog might be staying here and coming to the stables with me."

With a serious expression, Patrick nodded. "What kind of dog are you thinking about?"

"That's why I'm here. I'm not sure what route to take. It will need to be on the small side. Noelle's little, and I don't want her getting knocked over by a big, rambunctious animal. Plus, Gracie French will be spending a lot of time with it, and she'll need to be able to handle it, too."

"How small are we talking?"

Trent hadn't really thought about it. "I guess it depends. Not Chihuahua small. I have a physical job. It would need to keep up and handle being around horses in the event my brother doesn't keep it."

"Gotcha. We can rule out lap dogs." Patrick nodded. "If you're wanting a small breed, corgis are good with horses."

A corgi. He could picture it. "The girls would like a corgi."

"Or you could get a dachshund. They can be a handful, though, and they tend to want a lap to sit on."

"My hands are full enough at the moment. I don't need any more drama."

"A Pembroke corgi will suit your needs just fine. Those dogs love kids and are affectionate, but they're not as needy as some other small breeds. Plus, they're sturdy and have a natural tendency to herd horses. I advise you to get the dog acclimated to the stables and being around horses as soon as you get it, even if it will be spending most of its time at the house."

"Do you know where I can get one?"

"Do you want a puppy or a rescue dog?"

"Either is fine by me."

"How soon do you want it?"

"The sooner, the better. I have to get supplies first. And the girls and I will need to train it."

"I can help you with training." Patrick grinned. "Let me make a few phone calls. I have contacts all over the country. Someone will have the right dog for you."

"Thanks, Patrick. I appreciate it."

"I'll call you when I have more information."

Trent thanked him again and left. As he drove through town back to work, he thought about how much easier life was now that Gracie was taking care of the girls. They were all doing well in school and seemed to be adjusting fine. Emma still bossed everyone around. Sadie was really quiet, but maybe that was just her personality. And Noelle, while good-natured, continued to wake in the night. The light Gracie had bought helped somewhat, but he didn't know what else he could do to keep her from waking up.

Gracie had told the girl to pray. He felt foolish for not advising Noelle the same. Why hadn't he thought of that?

Yes, Gracie was in touch with their needs. He'd been surprised when she'd read her notes with all kinds of things to keep his nieces occupied, but it shouldn't have surprised him at all. She wasn't just a problem solver. She was a problem preventer.

He liked that she actively found alternatives to screen time. He also liked coming home to laughter and homework being finished. Made his life a whole lot easier than when Mrs. Pine had babysat.

He wished Kevin could see them all now. His brother had only managed one FaceTime session since they'd moved in, and the older girls might not mention it, but they missed him a lot. Noelle mentioned it often. She clearly was having the toughest time adjusting to Kevin being gone.

The Easter egg hunt would give them something else to think about. And a dog or a puppy would, too.

He turned down the road leading to the stables. Every day he watched for signs of spring. A few trees had begun to bud.

The stables were running smoothly. No lights had been left on since the night Cade had called. Jim and Elijah were handling all the weekend and night work, and that brought Trent some relief.

Trent supposed that's why he'd invited Gracie to join them at the Easter egg hunt, too. Having her help with the girls took another large burden from him. But was he being fair to her?

He'd been keeping their relationship professional from day one, yet he enjoyed her daily wrap-up regarding the girls. Didn't mind asking her for advice about things as they came up. But as much as he longed to develop a friendship with her, he'd been avoiding it.

Gracie was the type of girl he'd zoom right past friendship with—and he couldn't risk it.

His life as a bachelor might have shifted with the arrival of his nieces, but that didn't mean he was on the market for a girlfriend…or more.

Trent had enough going on, anyhow. Romance didn't work for him. He'd been hopeless at love most of his life. The few women he'd dated over the years had left dissatisfied within a few months. And they'd all said the same thing. *Horses are more important to you than I am.*

The sad thing was that they were right. The horses had been more important to him than the women he'd dated. Well, all but Elaine.

He'd given her more of his time than any other woman, and it still hadn't been enough.

Trent wasn't capable of keeping a girlfriend. And he didn't want one. He'd have to give up too much. He didn't see his commitment to his job going away anytime soon.

The horses relied on him. They trusted him. He understood what they needed without them saying it. And he'd never understood what women wanted, what they needed or how to make them happy.

He drove to the stables and cut the engine. Was this a good time to get a dog? The cold weather probably wouldn't let up for the next couple of weeks. Sometimes they got snowstorms in May.

There probably wasn't a perfect time to bring home a dog. He'd trust Patrick to let him know if a corgi was available, and he'd start researching them on his own tonight after the girls went to bed.

Inside the barn, Trent headed to his office. After checking emails and finishing up a few administrative tasks, he went in search of Jim and Elijah. He found Jim brushing one of the A-Team.

"How's everything going?" Trent asked.

"No complaints." Jim glanced over at him, then continued brushing the quarter horse. "Elijah's riding Gambit. I told him to ride Twixie after."

"Good." They currently boarded eight horses that needed to be exercised regularly. Trent loved riding them all, but he and Jim rotated with Elijah to make sure the horses were used to being handled by other people. That way they'd be ready for a variety of summer vacationers who'd be riding them. "I'm going to take Sarge out to the far pasture. See how it's holding up."

"As soon as the weather clears for good, we should move the A-Team to it."

"I hope it clears soon, but I'm not holding my breath."

"We'll get them in there by June at the latest."

The weeks would go by in a flash. Then the girls would be out of school for the summer. Trent didn't know what to think about that. He'd barely gotten used to the school routine. How different would it be in the summer?

He unlocked the tack room and hauled out everything needed to saddle Sarge, his gray thoroughbred. He'd bought him from his former boss in Kentucky. As a two-year-old, Sarge had been ruled out as a potential candidate for racing. He was a great horse, though. Smart, hardworking, fast and dependable. Trent considered the horse one of his greatest blessings. He strode out to the east pasture where Sarge and the A-Team roamed. His horse responded to his call, and soon, he had it saddled.

As they rode over the premises, he kept a watchful eye out. All of the pastures had shelter houses for the horses to huddle in during severe weather. Elijah and Gambit emerged from the trail in the woods and headed back to the barn. Six horses grazed in the other pastures. All of them were owned by locals. Trent kept the A-Team separate since he'd gotten them used to each other and never had any problems with them grazing together. He wanted to keep it that way.

As he made his way to the summer pasture, Trent's thoughts returned to Gracie. Her smile. Her laugh. Her way with his nieces.

She'd changed over the years. And for all his trying to

convince himself he wasn't capable of keeping a girlfriend, he still couldn't get her smile, her pretty hair or her nurturing personality off his mind. If he didn't watch out, he'd be in trouble.

"Is it ever going to warm up?" Gracie sat on Brooke's couch Friday evening. She'd said goodbye to the girls, verified what time Trent was picking her up tomorrow and driven straight to Brooke's. She didn't plan on staying long. Dean was picking up a pizza for their weekly movie night.

"Probably not." Brooke grinned, shrugging. "It is Wyoming."

"True. Are you and Dean taking the twins to the Easter egg hunt tomorrow?"

"Oh, yeah. They'll love it." She winced as she shifted to cross one leg over the other.

"How've you been feeling?" Gracie asked. With her rosy cheeks and ever-present smile, Brooke radiated good health. But she'd had a stroke two years ago, and she didn't take her health for granted. She'd even had her house renovated to be wheelchair accessible in the event she had another stroke.

"Pretty good. My leg was weak yesterday, so I've been taking it easy today." Brooke turned her attention to Alice, who was in the process of trying to reach something on the bookshelf. "Alice, no. We don't climb."

"Let me." Gracie got to her feet and went to the shelf. She smiled down at Alice. "What do you need?"

"Wock." She pointed to the large polished stone next to a stack of books.

"No," Brooke said, shaking her head. "The rock isn't a toy."

"How about this book instead?" Gracie pulled out a picture book from a lower shelf. "Ooh, look, it's a chicken."

"No chick." Alice crossed her arms over her chest and scowled. "Wock."

"Alice." Brooke's tone was a warning.

She stomped her little foot and began chanting, "Wock, wock."

"Sorry," Brooke said, sighing. "I'll handle this."

She went over to Alice and scooped her up. The toddler arched her back and began yelling and trying to break free from her grasp. "That's enough." Brooke hauled her out of the room and down the hall, leaving Gracie alone with Megan.

"How are you doing?" Gracie kept her tone sweet for the girl, but she turned and scampered off to follow her mother and twin.

Great. She'd scared the children. The way Alice was carrying on down the hall made her grateful she'd gotten older girls to babysit. Noelle sometimes got into a snit, but for the most part, all three were pretty easy.

Sadie was maybe too easy. She sensed the girl needed more attention. Her solitude and quiet nature made it simple to overlook her. She should mention it to Trent. Maybe the two of them could have a special outing. The other girls would get jealous, though. He *could* plan individual outings with each girl. She wouldn't mind babysitting the other two while he did. But he'd probably resent the suggestion— unless the special outing involved the horses in his care.

The stables clearly called his name. The girls knew the names of all the horses boarded there. Now and then, he loaded the girls in his truck right before closing time to make sure everything was in place at the stables. They thought of it as an adventure and always told her about it.

Gracie probably would have thought it was an adventure at their age, too.

"Sorry about that. Looks like I'm moving the rock out

of here." Brooke reappeared, carrying both twins. She lowered them to the ground and they sniffled their way over to the play corner. "Terrible twos. Hit this house like a hurricane, I tell you."

"You're great with them. You're a good mom."

Her eyelashes fluttered. "Thank you. That's awfully nice of you to say. I don't feel like a good mom when they throw tantrums."

"Part of growing up."

"How are the girls?" Brooke took her spot on the couch again. "And Trent? You two would make a great couple."

Her and Trent a couple? She wouldn't pretend she hadn't tried it on for size a time or two.

"The girls are great. Trent and I are not a couple."

"You could change that."

"No." She wasn't chasing after a boyfriend. Trent had shown no interest in her romantically, and it was probably for the best. They had a working relationship. Nothing more.

"Fine. But there aren't a lot of single guys around here. Trent and Ty are pretty much the only ones left."

"I'm not looking for a man, Brooke. You know that."

"Yes, but you aren't avoiding a man, either. If a good one came along, you'd at least consider him, right?"

"A good one hasn't come along and won't." She didn't want to get distracted by what-ifs. Her babysitting job paid great, and she loved it. But the year would fly by, and then she'd be right back to where she'd been a few weeks ago. Out of a job. And alone.

She would not get into a relationship until she'd taken steps to secure her future. That meant a full-time job with benefits. She'd wasted too many years relying on a boyfriend when she should have been relying on herself.

"You're just not in the right frame of mind. You need to join Christy Moulten's book club."

"She already gave me next month's book."

"Have you read it?" Brooke's face grew animated. "I'm on chapter seven, and I can't wait to finish."

"I haven't opened it yet." She liked the cover—a basset hound with a little boy—and the concept intrigued her. High school sweethearts reunited by a rescue dog and the man's young son. "I don't read many romance novels."

"I didn't, either, but Christy convinced me to try one. Now I can't get enough of them."

"Maybe that has something to do with your upcoming wedding."

"There is that." They both laughed. They discussed where Brooke was at with the wedding planning until Dean arrived. Gracie chatted with them both a few minutes and then let herself out. She drew her coat tighter as she walked to her car. Dusk had fallen, and she didn't want to go home to her empty apartment.

Maybe a supper out at Dixie B's was in order. Why not?

She drove home, parked her car and didn't bother going up to her apartment. The diner was only two blocks away. The cold air stung her face as she strode down Center Street. People were coming and going from the busy diner. When she arrived, Clem Buckley stood at the entrance and held the door open for her.

"You're in charge of Trent's young'uns, aren't you?" He made it sound like a crime. And even in the dim light, his gray eyes pierced her.

"Trent's nieces?"

"The three goldilocks."

"Yep."

"Well, get in there. It's too cold to stand out here all night."

He followed her inside. "He's not at the stables as much as he used to be."

"No?" She unwound her scarf and searched for an empty table. They were all occupied. Now she was stuck there talking to Mr. Grumpypants himself.

"No. He used to lock her up tight every night before the girls came along."

"I'm sure his staff is locking everything up just fine in his place."

"Are they?" Did the man ever blink?

"I don't know. I'm not involved with the stables."

"Humph." He gave her the side-eye and hitched his chin to a table opening up. "Come on. You might as well eat with me. It'll be a while before another table is available."

Eat with Clem? What a horrible thought. "Um, that's okay. I can wait. I've got time on my hands."

"Listen, Goldie—"

"It's Gracie."

"I know your name. You've got blond hair like Trent's girls, so you're Goldie, got it?"

She wasn't going to argue. She nodded.

"Unless you've got a hot date, I reckon you should join me."

"I haven't had a hot date in years and years."

His face softened, if such a thing was possible, and he jerked his thumb to the table. "Then you've got nothing to lose."

Nothing? She could lose plenty. Her appetite, for one. Her enthusiasm for the weekend, for another. But the aroma of burgers and fries hit her hard, and the way her stomach growled, she figured she might as well join the man.

"I guess I will. Thank you."

They made their way to the empty booth. An employee finished cleaning the table before they sat. Gracie scanned the menu. A waiter stopped by for their orders, and then Gracie settled into her seat and hoped Clem wouldn't frighten away her hunger for the double-cheeseburger she ordered.

"Your folks left years ago," Clem said. "Why are you back?"

She stretched her neck to the side until it cracked. "Brooke. She's my best friend. I missed her."

He nodded. "No job lined up first?"

"I thought I had one, but it fell through."

"What will you do when the young'uns go back with their daddy?"

"I'll find a full-time job. Probably something I can do from home."

"Home. Bah." He shook his head. "You need to be working with people."

"Well, there aren't oodles of full-time jobs around here."

He pointed to her, and her pulse took off like a frightened rabbit. "When the time comes, give me a call. I can put you in touch with any number of companies."

"Around here?"

"Yep. And the surrounding area. We take care of our own in these parts."

Our own. She hadn't really thought of herself in those terms, and it warmed her heart that Clem considered her one of them.

"Thanks, Mr.—"

"Clem. Just Clem."

"Thanks, Clem," she said softly, giving him a smile.

"Don't mention it. Word around town is you've been real good for those girls."

"They're darling. I just love them to pieces."

He nodded. "Do you ride?"

They discussed horses and rodeos until their food arrived, and when the meal was finished, they said their goodbyes. Gracie left with a full belly and a warm heart. She didn't feel as alone as she had earlier. Who could have imagined Clem Buckley would make her feel welcome? Maybe she really would be okay next year when the girls moved and she was left on her own. In the meantime, maybe she and Trent could be friends. No romance involved. She wasn't ready for it, and he didn't seem to want it—but friendship. They could do that. Couldn't they?

Chapter Six

Trent had never imagined driving with four females in his truck. And if he had, he certainly wouldn't have imagined enjoying it.

But he was enjoying it. Very much.

It made him nervous, too. All these random bits of conversation flying through the air. As soon as he began to make sense of one thread, a whole new one would start. How did they keep up with it all? His nieces and Gracie had a way of communicating he'd never master. As usual, he was clueless.

"Are you excited about finding lots of eggs?" Gracie, sitting next to him, twisted back—again—to talk to the girls. "I hope you get lots of chocolates and share some with me."

"I'll share mine with you!" Noelle's eager little voice made him smile.

"Me, too," Emma and Sadie said in unison.

His chest expanded at their sweet generosity.

"Did you hear that?" Gracie turned to him. "I'm getting chocolates."

Gracie French was a breath of fresh air in the dusty, locked closet of his life.

"What makes you think there will be chocolate?" he teased.

"This is Jewel River. There's bound to be chocolate." She switched back to the girls. "Are any of your friends going to be there?"

"Mrs. Christy's bringing Tulip." Noelle clapped her hands. "I can't wait to hug the doggie. I want a puppy!"

"Lindsey and Sophia are coming with their brothers and sisters," Emma said.

"What about you, Sadie? Will any of your friends be there?"

"I guess." Her quiet voice held no enthusiasm. While Emma reeked of self-assurance and Noelle's good nature shined bright, Sadie still didn't seem to be settling in.

As they discussed how they couldn't wait for summer to arrive, Trent pulled into Winston Ranch and followed the line of cars to the event center. The weather was clear but chilly. From the looks of it, half the town had turned out for this.

"Ooh, we're here!" Gracie pointed to the large pole barn where the egg hunt was taking place.

His heart took a tumble, and he didn't like it. But he liked her pretty face. It always seemed open, like she had nothing to hide, whereas he buried everything personal under fifteen layers.

Trent backed into a parking spot and cut the engine. Then he turned to address the girls. "Okay, here are the rules. We stay together. Let the younger kids have an egg if you find one at the same time—"

"We wouldn't steal an egg from a baby, Uncle Trent." Emma unbuckled her seat belt. "What kind of monsters do you think we are?"

"No one said anything about monsters." Leave it to Em to take his instructions in the worst possible way. Kids. He shook his head. Horses were so much easier.

Sadie climbed out of the truck and waited for Noelle to exit before shutting the door. Gracie herded Sadie and Noelle around the front of the truck to join him and Emma.

"Are we ready?" Gracie practically buzzed with excitement. "Let's get those eggs!"

Noelle held Gracie's hand, and Emma walked next to them, keeping up a steady stream of conversation as they went.

Trent put his arm around Sadie's shoulders. "Looks like we're partners for this. Since I'm tall, I can find some of the tougher-to-spot eggs."

"You don't have to help me."

"Who said anything about having to help? I want to help. Not that you need it. You've got all those detective skills from the books you've been reading."

"I did find out a new trick in a book I finished last week. Did you know you can pick locks with a special kit? It's this pouch that has teeny little metal rods in it. I really want one of my own."

Picking locks? What kind of books was she reading?

"Um, I'll have to look into it." He wanted to tell her that no way he was funding the start of her life of crime, but then he glanced at her and once more was struck by how small and quiet the seven-year-old really was.

"You mean it?" Her face brightened as she looked up at him.

He gave her a weak smile and said a silent prayer of gratitude that Gracie was holding the door open for them. For some reason, he'd always thought little girls were sunshine and dolls and sweetness. He hadn't been prepared for bossy, lock-picky and one that never slept.

Sadie slipped her hand in his, and they walked inside together. Unlike her sisters, she rarely initiated physical contact with him, and the gesture softened his heart.

Standing behind a table, Mary Corning and Angela Zane were handing out bags for the kids to keep their eggs.

"Well, look at this fine family." Mary beamed. "Gracie, with your blond hair, you could be these girls' mother. Trent, these little beauties are going to grow up to be heartbreakers."

"Don't I know it." He almost felt bad for Kevin. The teen years would be an adventure with these three.

Sadie let go of his hand to take a bag from Mary.

"See that line we taped over there?" Angela pointed to their left where fluorescent-orange tape stretched out on the floor. "The hunt will begin in fifteen minutes. Henry will make the announcement over the loudspeaker."

Emma spotted a friend and waved. "Can I go say hi to Lindsey?"

There went rule number one. Trent sighed. "Just for a sec. Then come right back."

As Emma scampered off, Gracie turned to Sadie. "If you see anyone you know, I'll go with you if you want to say hi."

"Tulip's here! Tulip's here!" Noelle yanked on Gracie's hand. "Come on!"

She met his gaze over the girls' heads. He hitched his chin. "Go ahead. Sadie and I will find a spot."

Noelle dragged her in the opposite direction, and Trent kept an eye out for Emma, currently chatting with a girl who had two brown braids.

"I don't want to get eggs." Sadie's blue eyes blinked up at him.

"Why not?" He made sure she was close to him as they made their way to a free spot near the orange tape on the floor.

"What if I grab one and it breaks open?"

"I'm sure a lot of them will. That's the point. You just scoop up the egg and candy and toss both in your bag."

"What if someone else gets one before I can pick it up?"

"Then they'll put it in their bag." He wasn't following her train of thought. "You'll go after another one."

"I don't think I'm cut out for this, Uncle Trent."

He crouched to her level and stared into her fear-filled eyes. "Why not? This isn't an Olympic event, Sadie. It's just a fun thing to do."

What was making her so scared? And how could he help her enjoy the egg hunt?

"What book were you reading last week that you liked so much?" he asked. She told him the name of it. "The main character—girl or boy?"

"Boy. Alexander."

"Would he think this is fun?"

"He's twelve. Too old for an Easter egg hunt."

Trent was running out of ideas. "Okay, let's say he had to be here. Say he had a younger sister. What would he do?"

"He'd sneak off to find clues."

"I don't want you sneaking off to find clues."

"Don't worry. There isn't a mystery to solve here. I have no reason to find clues."

Hmm. Maybe that was the angle to take. "How about we make the egg hunt a bit more interesting?"

"What do you mean?"

"I mean why don't we make our own rules? Here's mine. You have to find at least four eggs, and you get an extra point if one of them is purple." *Please, God, let me be handling her right. I don't know how to deal with these kids.*

"Do Emma and Noelle have the same rules?"

"No." A sense of confidence came over him. "This is just between you and me."

A small smile lifted her lips. "Okay. Four eggs. One purple."

"Where's Emma?" Gracie, with Noelle on her hip, squeezed in beside the family next to him. Her face was flushed. Man, she was pretty. But where was Emma? He stretched his neck to peer over the crowd.

"She should have come back by now." He looked at Sadie. "Stay with Gracie. I'll be right back." Without wasting a second, he weaved through the growing crowd to where he'd last seen her. He tamped down a sense of panic. He'd seen too many news stories about kids getting abducted. What if someone had snatched her?

"Uncle Trent!" He turned to the right. Relief almost weakened his knees. Emma darted between people to get to him.

"Where were you? I told you to come right back." He chastised himself for sounding so gruff.

"I know, but I had to go to the bathroom." Her face grew red.

He almost barked that she should have told him first, but he reined it in. "Come on, it's about to start."

Emma tugged on his hand. He glanced down at her.

"Are you mad at me?" Her eyebrows dipped together, and the worry in her expression softened his anxiety.

"No, Em, I'm not mad. I was worried. Didn't want you going missing."

Her face cleared. "Oh. I didn't think about that."

He bent to her level as people jostled them. "You're important, Emma. I'm going to keep tabs on you and your sisters the entire time you live with me. I won't let anything happen to you, but you have to listen to me."

She nodded. They made their way over to Gracie and the other two girls.

"I can't wait to get all kinds of candy!" Noelle was holding Gracie's hand while bouncing up and down.

"I know!" Gracie said. "Isn't this fun?"

He checked Sadie, and even she appeared to be somewhat excited about the hunt. He caught her eye and lifted four fingers. She nodded.

A voice over the loudspeaker announced for the children to take their places at the line. "Five, four, three, two, one. Go!"

The children surged forward. Trent tried to stay near Noelle since she was the smallest. An older boy reached for the egg she was picking up, and Trent stared down the kid until his face drained of color. The boy ran away. No one was taking Noelle's eggs. Not on his watch.

"You weren't thinking about beating up that little boy, were you?" Gracie drew close to him. He could barely hear her over the din of voices.

"If he takes her eggs? Maybe." He shrugged. She laughed, playfully smacking his chest with the back of her hand.

"You're terrible. Poor kid is probably going to have nightmares about you now."

"Good. It will make him think twice about taking things from a little girl."

He scanned the large space for Sadie and Emma. They weren't far from each other, and Sadie was actually climbing on top of a hay bale to reach an egg stuck in a potted plant. Good for her.

"It's nice to see her acting like a kid, isn't it?" Gracie asked.

"It sure is."

"Emma's always so mature. I feel like there's a thirty-five-year-old mom trapped in her body."

Emma? "I was talking about Sadie." He pointed to his middle niece. Her face lit with a smile as she crouched for another egg.

"She's having fun, too. Aww, that makes me happy." Gracie turned her attention back to Noelle, who'd raced ahead of them. "I'd better stay with her."

Trent chewed on what she'd said about Emma. Gracie was right. She did seem more like a mature adult than a nine-year-old. And Sadie had a hard time enjoying life the way her peers did. At least Noelle seemed to be a typical four-year-old. What did he know, though? He hadn't been around kids much.

Was he giving them what they needed? The last thing he wanted was for this year of their life to be a setback for them.

When the hunt ended, the girls joined him and Gracie at a long table and opened all their eggs. Sadie made sure to sit next to him and proudly showed him her haul. Nine eggs, and one of them was purple. He gave her a high five.

Gracie oohed and aahed over the candies, erasers, stickers and coupons they'd all gotten. As Trent looked at each of his nieces, he couldn't help thinking that this must be what being a family felt like. Noelle sat on Gracie's lap. Emma waved a coupon for a Dippity Doo ice cream cone, and Sadie was humming to herself as she arranged her goodies.

He wanted to hold on to this day. Hold on to this moment.

For as long as he could remember, he'd wanted to be part of a bigger family—not just the only child of a single mom working two jobs. And Gracie was the one who'd smoothed out the bumps and made it possible for his nieces to relax and enjoy themselves.

This wouldn't last. The girls would leave next year, Gracie would find her dream job—the one with all the benefits he couldn't give her—and he'd be back to devoting all his time and energy to the horses in his care. He should be happy about it, but part of him wanted to grasp the moment and never let it go.

"You have to come with us!" Emma tugged on Gracie's hand as they walked back to Trent's truck.

"Yeah, why don't you join us?" Trent glanced her way, and a shiver zipped down her body. His brown eyes shimmered with appreciation. She couldn't remember the last time a man had looked at her like that.

"Are you sure you don't want to have some time to yourselves?" Gracie wanted to agree but didn't want to intrude. A breeze blew a lock of hair across her face. She pushed it behind her ear.

"No! We want you to come." All three girls clutched their bags of goodies as they stared up at her with pleading eyes.

"Okay. Cowboy John's pizza, huh? Please tell me we're getting cheesy bread?"

"Oh, we're getting cheesy bread." He took her by the elbow to steer her away from a man not watching where he was going. She liked the feel of his hand on her arm and the tenderness behind it. The Winston was clearing out, and she wanted nothing more than to eat pizza with him and the girls.

"I want pepperoni!" Noelle skipped ahead. "I love pepperoni. Pepper-roni. Roni, roni, roni!"

"No mushrooms." Emma's bag swung back in forth in her hand. "We all think they're gross, right?" She gave stern stares to Sadie and Noelle.

"Eww, mushrooms." Noelle's lips curled under, and Sadie shook her head in disgust.

"Fine. No mushrooms." He pressed the fob to unlock the truck. "Although when I was your age, my mom told me I had to pick off anything I didn't like."

Gracie chuckled. "What did you end up picking off?"

"Green peppers. Nasty things." He held the passenger door open for her. "Who wants sausage? And ham? And bacon?"

"Me!" Noelle yelled, clutching her bag as she climbed into her booster seat.

"Me, too." Emma turned to Noelle. "Buckle up."

"Oh, yeah. I was eggsited."

"Excited. Ex. Not eggs." Emma rolled her eyes.

"Ex-cited." Noelle mimicked her, then stuck out her tongue. "Don't be mean."

"Sorry."

Trent shut their door and got settled into the driver's seat.

"Twenty-eight eggs." Sadie stared out her window. "That's how many we all got."

All the way back to town, the girls talked and laughed, and as soon as Trent parked, Gracie got out and helped herd the girls to the entrance. Cowboy John's had a small dine-in area with linoleum floors, weathered wooden tables and a row of booths along the side wall.

"Think we can fit in a booth?" Gracie asked him.

"Sure. The girls are small." He gestured for them to take a seat. "You guys can smoosh in on one side, right?"

They slid into the bench facing the back. Sadie sat near the window, Noelle was on her knees in the center, and Emma took the aisle seat. Gracie slid into the bench across from Sadie, and when Trent sat next to her, the hair on her arms prickled at his nearness.

She'd enjoyed watching him interact with the girls at the egg hunt. He'd tracked each one as best he could. A protective man. No pushover, that one. A guy like him could make a girl like her lose her head real quick.

She took the laminated menus lodged between the wall and the napkin holder and handed them out. "What are we thinking?"

"Two large meat-lovers and an order of cheesy bread." Trent didn't bother with a menu.

"Two large? That might be overdoing it." She'd seen Noelle and Sadie eat. She doubted they'd have more than a slice each.

"I'm starving. And we'll box up anything left over."

"Can we order sodas? What kind do they have?" Emma looked over her shoulder toward the dispenser behind the counter. Then she flushed and faced forward quickly.

"What's wrong?" Gracie asked her.

"Nothing." She seemed to shrink into her seat. Gracie stared beyond her where a family of four had walked in and were standing at the counter to place their order. A mom, dad and two boys. One appeared to be Emma's age.

"Yes, you can get sodas." Trent seemed oblivious to the undercurrents happening across from him. "But no refills."

"Oh, hey, Emma." One of the boys, the younger of the two, approached and stood next to their table. "Did you go to the Easter egg hunt?"

Noelle lifted up on her knees to talk to him. "I got lots of eggs!"

"That's cool." The skinny boy with brown hair grinned at Noelle. "I wish I could have gone. We had to visit my grandma in the hospital."

Emma's face returned to its normal color. "I'm sorry about your grandma. Is she okay?"

"Yeah. She got a new hip. She'll be home soon."

An employee approached to take their order. The boy returned to his family, who appeared to be ordering pizzas to go.

As Trent told the young woman their order, Gracie leaned forward to address Emma. "Who was that?"

Emma gave a quick glance over her shoulder to make sure he was out of earshot, then leaned in and whispered, "Braeden Jones."

"He's cute." Gracie sat back and nodded. "He seems nice."

"I like your friend," Noelle announced. "I'm gonna make his grandma a get-better card."

"Don't you dare." Emma turned to the girl in horror.

"What a nice idea." Gracie gave Emma a pointed stare. "His grandma would probably love a card from you. From all of you, actually."

Sadie shook her head. Emma did, too.

Gracie decided not to push it. Who knew what was going on in their minds?

Their drinks arrived, and all three girls plunked their straws into the takeout lids at the same time. Next to her, Trent checked his phone and seemed to relax.

"Good news. Your dad just let me know he'll be able to FaceTime with you tomorrow."

"Yay! Daddy!" Noelle clapped. "I miss him." She sank down, her smile collapsing.

Emma put her arm around the girl. "We all do. We'll see him tomorrow."

Sadie put her arm around her, too, and Gracie's heart tugged at the picture they presented. The three of them supporting each other.

"I wish we could FaceTime Mommy, too," Sadie said quietly.

Oh, dear. Gracie often forgot that they'd lost their mother only a few short years ago. Poor things.

"I wish your mommy was still here with you." Gracie met Sadie's eyes, then looked at the other two. "She'd be so proud of you." They shared a glance. "Emma, you're always looking out for your sisters, and you've adjusted to school in record time. And, Sadie, you're kind to everyone you meet, and you've already read fifteen books since moving here. Noelle, you have a big heart, and I wouldn't know what I'd do without your hugs."

"I like hugs." Noelle beamed.

"I do, too." Gracie checked Trent's reaction, hoping he wasn't mad at her for diving into a sticky situation.

"Gracie's right. Your mom would be proud of you." He cleared his throat. "Your dad, too. I know I am."

Their pizzas arrived, and Gracie helped the girls get the slices onto their plates. She tended to forget the girls were navigating life without their parents at the moment. It had to be tough on them.

She'd add these sweet girls to her prayers tonight. As Trent's muscular arm accidentally brushed hers, she tried not to react. She'd better add herself to those prayers, too. He was growing more attractive to her each day, and that wouldn't do.

Why worry about it? She'd enjoy a slice of pizza. Eating with Trent and the girls made her feel like she was part of a family. But she wasn't. And she'd have to continue to remind herself of that. Or next year, when they went back home, she'd be as droopy-eyed as Sadie had been when she'd wished her mom was there to FaceTime. And that wouldn't do at all.

Chapter Seven

"What are you talking about?" Trent rubbed the back of his neck the following Saturday night as he talked on the phone. The girls were upstairs playing, and he'd taken the opportunity to crash on the couch and channel surf, like he'd done in the old days before his nieces had arrived. Jim had called right before closing up the stables to let him know one of the local teens had pulled him aside with some concerns. "Why would any of us put manure in the stall? That doesn't even make sense."

"That's what I told him." Jim's gravelly voice sounded older than his sixty years. "I said, 'Don't blame us for not mucking out your stall.' But, Trent, something doesn't feel right about this. Colin and his brother are here every day taking care of their two horses. I just don't see them skipping out on chores and blaming us."

Trent didn't think so, either. "I'll come over. Check it out."

"Don't wake the little ones. I've already done a thorough check of everything. We're all set here. I'm leaving now."

He didn't tell him the girls were awake and would probably jump at the chance to do a walk-through of the barn. If Jim said he'd done a thorough check, Trent believed him. Still…he'd been overseeing the stables seven days a week before his nieces moved in. He hated not spending as much time there, especially on the weekends.

"Okay. Keep me posted if you hear or see anything else that isn't quite right."

"Will do." Jim ended the call.

Maybe Colin had forgotten to clean his stall. Things happened.

Trent's mind went back to a month ago when those lights had been left on. Were the two things related? Or with rodeo season in full swing, were some of the boarders getting forgetful?

Either way, it didn't matter. He was responsible for the property. It wouldn't hurt to check things out.

He forced himself to his feet and went to the bottom of the staircase. "Hey, girls? We need to go to the stables for a minute."

"Yay!" Noelle yelled. "Horsies!"

"Okay," Emma called. He could hear her talking to her sisters. "Get socks on. It's too cold for bare feet."

He headed to the mudroom and put on his work boots and coat. The girls ran in and shoved their feet into the new rain boots Gracie had helped them pick out. He got a kick out of their choices. Noelle's were pink with puppy faces. Emma's were plain yellow. And Sadie's were blue with little daisies.

"Ready?" He didn't bother telling them to zip up their coats. They wouldn't be gone long, and if the girls got cold, they were smart enough to zip them on their own.

"Yes." They headed outside and got settled in his truck. In no time, he'd entered the alarm code and unlocked the stable door. He flipped on the lights as the girls raced ahead.

"I want to see Twixie!" Emma reached the main aisle and turned right to where the A-Team were in their stalls for the night.

"I like Bear." Sadie turned in the opposite direction to where the locals kept their horses.

And Noelle reached for Trent's hand. "Uncle Trent?"

"Yes, sweetheart?" His gaze took in everything, trying to see if anything appeared out of the ordinary.

"When I get older, I want a pony."

"I don't blame you."

"But first, I want a puppy."

Trent had to bite his tongue. She asked for a puppy every day. Little did she know in less than twenty-four hours—tomorrow, Easter Sunday—she'd be holding a corgi puppy.

Patrick had called him on Wednesday to let him know a breeder had sold a litter, but at the last minute, one of the families had backed out, leaving a lone boy pup without a home. Trent had put a deposit down immediately, and Patrick—already driving to pick up two dogs for his training center—had brought the puppy back with him today. After church tomorrow, Trent and the girls would meet him at the training center to pick it up.

"I know. You've mentioned a puppy a time or two." He pointed down the aisle. "Let's go check on Opie."

"Okay." She skipped ahead. "Why did they name him Opie? Is he the white one with the big brown circles? I like that one."

"No, he's the brown one with the white cross on his forehead."

"Oh, right. There are two horsies like that. Do you think Jesus put the cross on them to remind him of Easter? I like Easter. I can't wait to find my basket."

"Find your basket?" What did she mean? He'd purchased three baskets, a bunch of toys and candy, but he wasn't sure what to do with it all. Anxiety mounted as they strolled, and he grabbed the handle of each stall door to make sure they were all locked.

"Yes! The baskets hide on us. Mine was in the dryer last year, and Emma had to help me find it."

Trent wished he had asked Kevin more questions during their FaceTime last Sunday. The girls had been so excited to tell him everything that had happened since he'd last called, Trent hadn't had the heart to cut them off. Afterward, Noelle had cried in his arms about how much she missed her daddy, and Sadie had gotten awfully quiet. Emma had gone straight to her room.

Living with him was tough on them. He and Gracie had discussed it this week, and he hadn't realized they were grieving their mom and missing their dad so much. He'd been praying for direction with the girls. At least Gracie made life better for them. She knew what they needed, unlike him.

Sadie shoved her fingers in the open window of a stall door and hoisted herself to peek through the bars. "Hi, Bear."

The horse made a snuffling sound and came over to her. She giggled. Trent tucked away that happy sound. He didn't hear Sadie laugh all that often. He hoped he'd hear more of it as time wore on. Up ahead, he found Colin's horse.

"Hello, Opie." The horse turned at his voice and approached the door. After unlocking the stall, Trent instructed Noelle to stay in the aisle while he went inside, closing the door behind him.

He talked softly to Opie and ran his hand gently down his neck. His stall had been one of the tidiest since Moulten Stables opened. Colin and his brother, Jacob, showed up every morning before school and came back every afternoon. If one of them had something going on, the other took care of both their horses.

"Everything looks good in here now." Trent studied the

space as he lavished attention on Opie. "Wish you could talk and tell me if anything's been going on in your stall."

The horse shook its mane, and Trent chuckled. "You'd have plenty to say, wouldn't you?"

He went back to the aisle and locked the door behind him. Noelle had found a seat on an overturned bucket and had plopped her little elbows on her thighs and let her chin drop into her cupped hands.

"What's wrong?"

"Emma and Sadie don't want me around."

"Well, I want you around. Come on, partner. Let's check the rest of the stalls."

She brightened, and Trent hauled her up onto his hip and carried her from stall to stall so she could see the horses. At the end of the aisle, a set of doors led outside. To the left were restrooms and the locals' tack room with individual lockers. To the right was a large open area that ended in double barn doors where they led the horses out to the training arena, trails and pastures. He carried Noelle to the doors and looked out the windows.

"Why is that wheelbarrow over there?" she asked.

"Good question." He followed her finger to the wheelbarrow next to the large barn, where they kept feed, hay and equipment. "Someone must have forgotten to put it away."

"It looks stinky." She turned away from the window and held her nose between her finger and thumb.

Trent peered at it. Noelle was right. Whoever had last used it hadn't rinsed it down. And they hadn't put it away in the barn, either. Tension wound his muscles. There were rules here for a reason.

"Let's go take care of it." He set her on her feet.

"Can I go see the horses with Emma and Sadie instead?"

"Sure." It would only take a few minutes to put away the

wheelbarrow. He headed outside. After a quick spray with the hose, he moved the wheelbarrow into the barn next to the others and locked up.

Cade had installed outdoor security cameras in the parking lot near the stables' entrance. But the rest of the property—the outbuildings, paddocks, pastures, trails and training arena—were only accessible from the stables. Cameras weren't installed anywhere else.

Trent would have to talk to the teens on Monday about the rules again. Did they have any newer boarders? He couldn't think of any off the top of his head. The teens who had horses here were all grateful to finally have a place nearby to board them. Most had been wanting to be on the rodeo team for a while, but they'd had to board their horses too far away to make it feasible. Moulten Stables, being only five minutes from the high school, had made all of these kids' rodeo dreams possible, and they showed their appreciation by treating the facility with respect. It helped that Cade had given them rock-bottom low rates, too.

Back inside, he found the girls lavishing attention on Granite through the stall door. When Noelle spotted him, she raced to him. "See, Uncle Trent? Granite has a white cross just like Opie."

"He sure does." But Granite was two hands taller than Opie and quite a bit stronger, too. No one would ever mix up those two. "Okay, ladies, I'm done here. Ready to head back?"

Within minutes, they were in his truck keeping up a steady stream of conversation about their favorite horses and how much they wanted to learn how to ride. Trent planned to teach them this summer.

"I don't want to ride a big horse," Noelle declared, kicking her legs from her booster as he pulled into the driveway. "I want a nice, pretty pony."

"Me, too." Sadie nodded.

"Not me," Emma said. "I want a white horse. And I'll braid her hair with ribbons and ride her in a parade."

"Ooh, I want to braid my horsie's hair with ribbons!" Noelle clapped her hands.

"No copying."

Trent cut the engine and waited for them to get out. In the mudroom, they pulled off their boots. "Put everything where it belongs."

He gave them the same reminder every day. They were getting better at lining up their shoes and boots on the mats and hanging up their coats on the hooks on the wall.

"I can't wait to get my Easter basket tomorrow." Emma's eyes shined. "And wear my new dress."

"I love my new dress. It's so pink!"

"I like mine, too," Sadie said softly.

"Well, girls, we've got a busy day tomorrow, so go upstairs and get ready for bed." He tensed, waiting for them to argue, as they usually did.

"Okay!" The trio ran upstairs, laughing and talking all the way.

That was fast. And oddly easy. He rubbed his chin.

Now what to do about the Easter baskets? He wasn't sure how to put them together. And where was he supposed to hide them?

Shaking his head, he did the only thing a sane bachelor would. He called Gracie.

She'd know what to do.

Trent wanted her help? Gracie's spirits soared. She'd been sitting in her apartment, terribly bored, when he'd texted her to ask for advice. His short text didn't make much sense, but she assumed he needed help with the Easter basket situation, so she'd offered to come over. She'd half expected him to turn her down, but he'd texted THANK YOU in all caps, and that amused her. She wouldn't deny it felt good to be needed.

She glanced around his porch after she'd texted him that she was at the front door. He opened it and swept her inside.

"Thanks for coming. I told them they had to stay in their rooms even if they weren't sleeping."

"And they've obeyed?" She unwound her scarf and unzipped her coat.

"So far." He took her coat and hung it on the back of a chair in the dining room. They headed to the living room, where bags full of stuff had been strewn all over the carpet. He ran his fingers through his hair. "I don't know what I'm doing."

She hoped there were three baskets in there somewhere.

"Let's see what you've got." She knelt on the carpet and opened one of the bags. Trent plunked down beside her, hitting her with the scent of leather and soap. *Oh, boy.* He smelled really good.

"Noelle said their baskets are hidden every year. Kevin never told me that. I'm just going to throw everything in the baskets and hope for the best." He jerked open the bag to his right.

"You will do no such thing." She kept her voice low but couldn't keep the scolding out of it. "You already did the hard part—buying everything. Putting the baskets together will be simple."

"You know what you're doing then?" The way his eyebrows drew together almost made her laugh.

"Relax, cowboy. This isn't advanced calculus." She pulled out everything and asked him who got what. He pointed to bags upon bags of candy, three stuffed animals—horses, of course—sticker books, walkie-talkies and other toys. Had he purchased the entire supercenter from the next town over? "Um. Wow."

"I didn't know what to buy." His voice had a panicky element. "So I just threw everything in the cart. Did I get it all wrong?"

Sympathy for him flooded her. "You've never been around little girls, have you?"

"No, I've spent most of my life around guys and horses. That's it."

"Nothing wrong with that." She hadn't realized how in over his head he was with things she took for granted. "You did good. But this is too much. Why don't we set aside some to give to them later on? You know, for their birthdays or on one of those days when everyone's ornery and bored and desperately in need of something new."

"Desperately in need of something new" described herself today. After an early morning coffee session with Brooke and the twins at Annie's Bakery, Gracie had faced a long day alone. And this after every weeknight alone.

She'd never thought she'd feel lonely by moving back here, but she did. Probably because her friends had full lives. She didn't begrudge them that, but she didn't have a boyfriend to hang out with or kids of her own to raise or a chocolate shop to run or any of the other things that filled their days and nights.

"Smart thinking." He nodded and cracked his knuckles. At least she had the girls and Trent. Every weekday morning, she looked forward to arriving at the farmhouse. She'd chat for a minute with him before he left for work, then she'd hang out with Noelle all day and pick up the girls. The following two hours were hectic and fun while she helped with homework, listened to their days, gave advice and started a simple supper to make life easier for Trent. Most of the time, she ate with them.

Her little family.

Except they weren't really hers.

She sighed.

"Asking you to help is too much, isn't it? I shouldn't have called you so late. And on your day off. Just tell me what to do with all this and you can be on your way. I'm sorry."

"What? No. I wasn't busy, and I actually love doing this sort of thing."

"Then what's wrong?"

She was surprised he'd picked up on her mood.

"Nothing. I'm glad you called. I was feeling lonely."

"Oh." He held a package of pink plastic grass. "You're lonely here?"

"No." She shook her head, stacking bags of candy on the floor in front of her. "Saturdays get to me sometimes, though."

"Really? I would have thought you'd be thrilled to have a break. A whole day for yourself."

"The morning is usually great because I hang out with Brooke. But then I'm left to my own devices. My apartment takes all of twenty minutes to clean, and that leaves me…" Unsure what to do with herself. She needed a hobby. Or two. "What did you do on your Saturdays before the girls moved in?"

His face softened. "I spent all day at the stables. I'd tackle all the maintenance work that needs to be done regularly. And I'd check every horse. Make sure the A-Team was getting extra trail rides."

"You miss it, don't you?" The man loved his job. "The extra time with the horses and working on the stables?"

"I do." His shoulders fell as reality settled on him. "The

girls and I went over tonight to check on everything. I wish I could go every night like I used to."

"Cade was pretty smart hiring you." She pressed up from a kneeling position to bring the empty baskets to her spot.

"Why do you say that?"

"You love what you do, and you give it all you've got."

He gave her a sharp glance. Was it something she'd said? She eyed him warily. "What? Did I say something wrong?"

"No. I'm just surprised, I guess. You said that like it was a good thing."

"Why wouldn't it be?" She waited for him to answer, but the moment passed.

"What do I do with this?" He opened the pink grass and held up a handful.

"Start spreading it in the bottom of each basket. Here." She handed him the first one. "Let's fill them assembly-line style."

He did as he was told, but the fact that he didn't answer her question bothered her.

"What's wrong with loving the horses and your job?" She tried to open a bag of jelly beans, but the plastic wouldn't budge. "Do you have a knife or scissors?"

"Here. Let me." He took the bag from her, and his fingers brushed hers. Big, strong hands. A tiny, swoony sigh escaped. She hoped he hadn't heard it. He handed the bag, now opened, back to her, and the vulnerability in his eyes made her want to comfort him—for what, she didn't know.

"I'm sure it won't come as a surprise to you that I haven't dated many women."

She wasn't surprised by the fact. What she wanted to know was why. Why didn't he have a line of single women ready and eager to date him?

"I, uh, I've been accused of being married to my job. Showing the horses more affection than my girlfriend."

"Oh." Her heart squeezed. The words had clearly cut him deeply. "What was her name?"

"Wasn't just one." His shoulder lifted. "They all said the same thing."

"But one in particular mattered, didn't she?"

He shifted to face her. "Elaine. And, yeah."

"I'm sorry. You should never have to apologize for loving your job and doing it well."

"Yeah, well, I don't blame her for breaking things off. I *am* more dedicated to my job than most women can handle. It's not a nine-to-five for me. It's my life. The horses and the grounds mean more to me than any woman ever could."

Gracie couldn't pretend the words didn't deflate her ego a bit. "You've found a way to raise the girls and take care of the horses."

"Only because I have to." His defensive tone was hiding something. "Not by choice."

"You're doing a good job."

"Not really." He faced her then and met her gaze. "I can't seem to turn it off. At night, I wish I had the freedom to go over there at any hour like I used to. But when I'm with the girls, I forget that Elijah and Jim are shutting it all down. Makes me wonder if I'm losing my edge."

"You're not losing anything. You're juggling a lot. I, for one, think you're handling it all well." She began placing equal amounts of candy in each girl's basket. But she felt Trent's stare and glanced up. The intensity in his gaze lifted the hair on her arms.

"Thank you," he said. "For the encouragement, for coming over and for everything you're doing with the girls. They're happy. It's because of you."

Heat rose up her neck. "They're easy to love. I enjoy my time with them."

Her eyes met his, and they shared a moment of under-standing…and more. Did he ever think of her romantically? She'd been thinking of him romantically. Way too often. She shouldn't think of him like that at all.

"What next?" He grabbed one of the stuffed horses. "These?"

"Not yet. Let's get the other stuff in here first."

They spent the next hour filling and hiding the baskets, laughing and talking the entire time. When they finished, Gracie put on her coat and shoes, and Trent walked her to the door.

"Would you like to sit with us at church tomorrow?" he asked.

"Really? I'd love that."

"We're driving to Patrick's training center right after to pick up the you-know-what. You're welcome to join us."

"I want to be there. I can video the entire thing."

"I'd appreciate it." The way he was staring made her think he might want to kiss her. A light went out in his eyes. "See you tomorrow."

She gave him a weak smile and left. Under a sky full of stars, Gracie barely registered the cold air. Tonight had been unexpected in the best possible way. And tomorrow, she'd get to do it all over again. She couldn't wait. Even if Trent was giving her mixed signals.

Chapter Eight

❧

"I love my new pony!" Noelle twisted and shoved her stuffed animal in Gracie's face for the fifth time since the final hymn had been sung in church. Trent made a mental note to have a talk with Noelle about personal boundaries. But Gracie seemed to be taking it like a champ. Noelle sat on her lap and pretended to make the horse trot through the air. The ushers were still letting out the front rows.

He'd taken the spot on the aisle. Emma sat to his right, Sadie sat next to her, with Noelle and Gracie on her other side.

"What are you going to name it?" Gracie whispered.

"I don't know." Noelle didn't lower her voice. "Prancer?"

Emma leaned forward and shook her head. "That's a reindeer name, Noelle. You can't name it that."

"Okay, let's wait until we're out of church before naming the horses." Trent looked around to see if anyone seemed miffed about the girls' talking. At least all three had been quiet, if squirmy, throughout the service. He realized everyone was chatting with their neighbors. No need to worry.

"You can name your pony anything you want." Gracie smoothed her hand over Noelle's hair. Then she turned to Sadie. "What are you naming yours?"

"Moonlight." She wrapped her arms around the stuffed animal and hugged it tightly.

55555555555

"I like that name. What made you decide on it?" Gracie picked up Noelle and helped her on her feet. The ushers were nearing their pew. Trent made sure nothing had fallen to the floor before stepping out so the girls and Gracie could exit in front of him.

"I woke up last night and saw the moonlight on the horse pastures across the road," Sadie said as she fell in line behind Emma. "It looked really pretty. And my horse is pretty, so I think moonlight is just right."

Wow. He couldn't remember ever hearing so many words come out of Sadie's mouth at once. Gracie hoisted her purse strap over her shoulder and guided Noelle to where Trent stood. "Perfect name. Very meaningful."

All five of his senses had gone on high alert the moment Gracie passed by him. Her modest blue dress and cardigan brought out the blue in her eyes. Her soft sweater brushed his arm. Her perfume was light and fresh—just like her—and her gentle tone softened his rough edges.

What if this was his actual life? What if he had a wife and three daughters? Sunday church with his own family?

He gulped and followed them out of the sanctuary. They reached the large entryway, where everyone was talking, and the girls went over to Christy Moulten, who raved about their pretty dresses. Erica and Dalton brought their kids over to join them. Then Cade and Mackenzie came by, and Brooke, Dean, Dean's father Ed, Anne and the twins were right behind them.

All of them were in various stages of being a family.

"Guess what?" Brooke took Gracie by the arm. Trent kept his ears open.

"What?"

"Reagan went into labor early this morning!"

"Really?" Gracie's mouth dropped open, and her eyes lit like stars.

Trent could watch her sparkling eyes all day.

"Yeah, just think. In a few hours, I'll get to meet my niece or nephew!"

He'd never thought he could have a family. Or that he was meant for one. Or that he could hold on to a family if by some chance he got one.

Maybe he was wrong.

"Trent?" Mackenzie motioned for him to come over. He hitched his chin to her as they scooted off to the side.

"What's up?"

"My mother asked my dad to attend church with her at the last minute. They're divorced, but he still tries to watch out for her. Anyway, she lives almost two hours away, and he asked me to tell you to come over in a few hours. I hope that doesn't ruin your day."

"No, no, not at all." He mentally recalculated the plan. "It will give me time to get the girls changed and fed."

"Oh, good." She sighed in relief. "I know how excited you must be."

"I am. Not as much as those three will be, though." He glanced back and noted the circle of people was breaking up. Gracie approached, holding Noelle's hand. As Gracie and Mackenzie chatted, he found the girls' coats and helped put them on over their dresses.

"Slight change of plans." Trent met Gracie's gaze above the girls' heads. "We're going to change out of our church clothes and have some breakfast."

She seemed to understand. "Why don't you guys come over to my place after you change? I'll cook a big breakfast for you."

"I want to see your house!" Noelle began bouncing.

"I do, too." Emma grinned.

"Me, too." Sadie hugged her horse and smiled.

"I don't want to put you out." Trent didn't know how wise it would be to spend time at her place. He was already having foreign thoughts about families and watching her sparkly eyes and what-not. His collar grew tight.

"You wouldn't be putting me out." She laughed, and the sound was like little bells. "I invited you, remember?"

"Come on, Uncle Trent!" Emma tugged on his hand.

"Please?" Sadie's big eyes blinked up at him.

"Okay. We'll change and come over in, say, thirty minutes?" He rubbed the back of his neck. This wasn't in his plans for the day.

"Great. Park behind the building. There's a door in the back that leads up to my apartment. I'll be waiting for you."

"Sounds good." Too good. He didn't think he could take much more domestic closeness with the woman. He really should have said no.

All the way back home—all four minutes—the girls speculated about what Gracie's place would look like. He tried to tune it out. But he had to admit, he was curious about her apartment, too.

While the girls changed into jeans and sweaters, he mentally checked through his list for bringing the puppy home. He'd bought baby gates to keep the pup in one area. The food and toys he'd ordered had arrived a few days ago. Patrick was supplying a crate, collar and leash.

Ready or not, Trent was only a few hours away from bringing home a dog. Could he handle it? What if the dog hated him? What if he wasn't good at caring for a puppy? What if the dog ran away? Or, worse, died?

He went to the kitchen table and gazed at the backyard.

Everyone he loved seemed to leave too early, either by choice or by dying.

"What's wrong, Uncle Trent?" Sadie stood next to him. He hadn't heard her approach.

"Oh, nothing." He gave his head a slight shake. "I was just missing some people."

"Like who?"

He patted his lap and she sat on it. "My mom. She died a long time ago, and I miss her."

"I miss my mom, too. And my dad. What was your dad like?"

"I don't know." He rested his chin on the top of her head. "He died when I was little."

"I hope my daddy doesn't die."

"He's not going to, sugar."

She twisted back to look at him. "How do you know?"

"I don't know for sure. But we'll pray for God to protect him. And if anything ever happens to him, you'll always have me."

"Promise?"

"Promise." He kissed the top of her head. The other girls came in, arguing about something. They argued about a lot of things, and he ignored most of it. "You guys ready to go?"

"Yeah!"

"Coats and sneakers, okay?"

"Why sneakers?"

"Cuz I said so."

"That's not a real answer." Emma had one hand on her hip.

"It's my answer. Deal with it."

She let out a humph. They got back into his truck. All the way to Gracie's, he thought about how the weather would be warm enough for shorts soon. The grass would green up, and it would be blue skies and sunshine.

In no time, they arrived at Gracie's and parked.

"Be careful on the steps, and knock when you get up-stairs." Trent held Noelle's hand as the other two climbed the stairs ahead of them.

"You're here!" Gracie opened the door and waved them inside. The first thing Trent noticed was how bright the apartment appeared. The front window let in a lot of light. The second? It smelled like bacon, sausage and pancakes—and he loved all three. Finally? There was a whole lot of pink.

Pink pillows on the couch. A pale pink fluffy throw over a wooden rocking chair. Pink pots holding houseplants. There was even a pink porcelain bunny figurine on the end table.

"You really live here?" Emma's eyes widened as she took it all in. "This is the best place ever."

He frowned. He'd thought the farmhouse was the best place ever.

"Hey, I can see the chocolate shop from here." Sadie stood in front of the large front window overlooking Center Street.

"It's so pink!" Noelle had taken the pink throw and wrapped it around herself. "I love your pink blankie—it's like mine!"

Trent cleared his throat. "Girls, let's get those shoes off and see what Gracie needs help with."

Gracie, holding a spatula, had returned to the kitchen. She caught his eye, scrunched her nose and winked. "If you girls could set the table for me, that would be a big help. I have the plates and silverware out already."

Emma raced over and hefted the plates off the counter. "These have bunnies on them."

"I know. Aren't they great?" Gracie flipped pancakes on an electric griddle. "I found them at a thrift store last year, and I thought they would make Easter even better."

"Let me see!" Noelle ran up to Emma, who was setting the

plates around the table and showed her one. "Oh, and there are flowers on them, too. We get to eat pancakes on bunnies."

Sadie came over and agreed they were by far the best plates they'd ever seen. As the girls distributed the silver-ware and paper napkins, Trent eased into the small kitchen. "Anything I can help you with?"

He never should have entered it. The kitchen couldn't be bigger than the photo booth Cade and Mackenzie had rented for their wedding. With Gracie so close, he had the urge to wrap his arms around her.

"The syrup and butter are right behind you," she said brightly. "Could you put them on the table for me?"

"Sure thing." He wanted to linger, to lean over her shoul-der and inhale the sweet scent of the pancakes. He also wanted to run out of there all the way to his truck. This situation with Gracie confused him. Was the abundance of pink messing with his head? Or was it hunger for breakfast?

She was the girls' nanny. But she was also his sounding board. And his friend. She'd helped him in so many ways.

He set the syrup and butter in the center of the table, which had a pink-and-green-checked tablecloth. Of course. More pink. He backed up two steps. He didn't belong here. It was too cozy, too feminine. Too tempting. A part of him wanted to sit on her couch and soak it all in for hours.

"We're all set!" Gracie held a platter of bacon and sausage. He took it from her, and she returned with a large plate of pancakes. The girls found seats at the table. "Trent, would you mind saying the prayer?"

Yes, he'd pray. Pray that God would relieve him of this attraction to her.

Everyone bowed their heads. "Lord, we thank You for this Easter Sunday. Thank You for saving us from our sins and promising us eternity with You. And thank You for this food."

"Amen."

Gracie looked at Sadie, sitting next to her. "Would you like bacon?"

"Yes, please, and sausage."

Trent stacked three pancakes on Noelle's plate and gestured for Emma to give her plate to him. As everyone drizzled syrup over their pancakes and nibbled on the breakfast meats, the conversation returned to Gracie's apartment.

"When we're finished eating, I'll give you the tour," she said. "It's not big, though."

The three girls exchanged excited glances. He didn't need the tour. He already felt like he'd landed in a pink, girly dream.

She was fluffy throws and bunny plates and pink pillows.

He was dirty boots and saddles and leather.

They were incompatible. Plain and simple.

But at the moment, he was sure glad he had her—for the girls' sake. Maybe being surrounded by pink was exactly what his nieces needed after not having a mom for two years.

And maybe he needed a little bit of it, too.

"Where are we going?" Emma asked for the fourth time. Gracie, sitting in the passenger seat of Trent's truck, glanced at him with a smirk. After their pancakes, she'd given him and the girls a tour of her apartment. Noelle had climbed onto her bed and declared she wanted to sleep in it forever. Emma had agreed it was the prettiest bedroom she'd ever seen, and Sadie said she wanted the exact same room, only in pale blue.

Those girls. They were the sweetest things.

All three loved the straw cowboy hats she'd gotten them for Easter presents and were currently wearing them.

Gracie hadn't been prepared for the effect having Trent in

her apartment had had on her. His large frame had dwarfed every room he'd been in. And his leathery scent had followed him wherever he went. When she'd showed the girls her bedroom, he'd stood in the doorway, looking extremely uncomfortable and out of place. He'd shifted his weight from one foot to the other and excused himself to the living room. Not long after, he'd declared it was time for the girls to get their shoes on because he had a surprise for them. And Gracie was coming with.

She liked that he'd made a point to include her. Between last night and church this morning, she'd worried he'd change his mind about her joining them to pick up the puppy. And she'd definitely been getting an unsettling vibe from him ever since he'd stepped into her apartment.

Maybe all the beige had bothered him. She'd tried to offset the neutral tones with pastel pinks to brighten it up, but there was only so much she could do with a rental.

"Can't you just tell us?" Emma sounded peeved.

"You'll see." Trent's eyes danced with anticipation. He drove into the training center parking lot. "Everybody out."

"What's this place?" Sadie asked.

"It's where Mr. Howard teaches dogs," Emma said as they stepped onto the pavement. "My teacher said he trains dogs for people who need help."

"What kind of people?" Noelle skipped next to her, and Sadie caught up to them.

"People with disabilities."

Trent made sure all the doors were shut and headed to the entrance.

"Why are *we* here?" Emma asked.

"You'll see," he said.

Gracie could practically feel the thrum of the girls' nerves—anticipation mixed with fear. The fear would be chased away soon enough. She got the camera ready on her phone. She didn't want to miss a second of their response when they found out why Trent had brought them there.

Inside, Patrick was waiting for them. He grinned and waved everyone over. "Ah, you made it. Sorry about having to delay this."

"No problem. Mackenzie told me you were attending church in another town." Trent shook his hand. "Thank you for meeting us here—on a holiday, no less."

"I live for this sort of thing." Then Patrick addressed the girls, standing in a row. "Do you know why you're here?"

In silence, they shook their heads.

"Today is a very special day. I heard you girls like dogs."

"I love dogs!" Noelle clapped her hands.

"We do, too, don't we, Sadie?" Emma said, nudging her sister with her elbow. Sadie, wide-eyed, nodded.

"Good. Good." He turned and hitched his chin for them to join him. "Come with me."

The older girls exchanged curious glances, and Noelle raced beside Patrick. Gracie prepared to start recording.

"Wait here, okay?" Patrick led them into one of the enclosed training areas. "I'll be right back."

"What's going on?" Emma stood near Trent. "What's he doing?"

"Wait and see." Trent nodded for her to join her sisters, both on their knees on the training mat.

When Patrick came back, holding a puppy, Gracie began recording.

"This is a Pembroke corgi." He petted the pup in his arms. "He's almost ten weeks old. And he's going to live with you from now on. Your uncle decided it was time to get a dog."

Noelle's shock turned to awe as she held her arms out. "He's ours? A puppy?"

Emma turned to Trent with her forehead furrowed. "This isn't a trick, is it?"

"I would never trick you, Emma." Trent pulled her into his arms and hugged her. "This is our new dog."

Tears began pouring out of her eyes.

Sadie hadn't moved. Gracie paused the recording and went over to put her arm around her shoulders. "Are you okay, Sadie?"

Only then did the girl snap out of it. "We really get to have a puppy? This puppy?"

Gracie nodded, smiling tenderly at her.

Sadie launched herself into her arms and sobbed. Gracie hadn't realized the girls would be so emotional. She'd thought they'd be thrilled, but they all seemed to be overwhelmed. Well, except Noelle. She'd raced to Patrick and was currently sitting on the mat and trying to hold the tiny, wiggly pup.

"I love him. I love him!" Noelle couldn't contain her excitement. "He's so soft. And look at his face. He has a white line on his forehead like the horsies at the stable. Oh, this is the best day ever!"

Emma and Sadie rushed over to inspect the puppy, and Gracie resumed her video. The puppy was tan with white paws and a white stripe on its forehead. Its fuzzy body and big ears made him even more adorable than the average pup.

As the girls oohed and aahed over the dog, Patrick explained what they needed to do to take care of him. They listened as well as they could while the puppy tumbled in and out of their laps. Finally, it was time to go.

Trent carried the supplies to the truck. Gracie held the puppy, and the girls crowded her as they crossed the parking lot.

"What are we going to name him?" Emma asked.

"Can he sleep in my bed?" Noelle asked.

"How big is he going to get?" Sadie asked.

Trent tried to answer as best as he could. Soon enough, everyone got settled and he started the truck. Gracie kept the puppy on her lap. He seemed so small and full of energy. Trent turned to her. "You still want to come over for a bit? Help us get him used to his new home?"

"I'd love to."

"I can drop you off at your apartment if you have something else to do."

"I don't have anything else going on. Besides, it's not every day I get to hang out with a puppy. I want to come over."

"You'll be spending a lot of days with this little guy from now on." He chuckled and began to drive.

"Uncle Trent, can we name him?" Emma asked.

"I think we should call him Skippy," Noelle said.

"That's a dumb name." Emma sounded annoyed.

"It's not dumb!"

Gracie intervened. "Maybe you could each write a name for the puppy on a paper, and we could have a drawing." She glanced back, but the girls didn't seem to like that idea much.

"Good idea," Trent said.

"Okay. We'll each choose a name." Emma gave the girls a thumbs-up. "We're on it."

Gracie wasn't surprised. For all the arguing they were capable of, those three showed remarkable team effort at times. And, clearly, this was one of those times.

When they got back to the farmhouse, Trent hauled the supplies inside. Gracie and Noelle tried to get the puppy to go potty. When the pup took too long, Noelle hauled her Easter basket outside, distracting the little dog with colored eggs until he did his business. Finally, they joined the other two girls at the table and started writing down names. Trent had gated off the kitchen area to keep the dog from wandering throughout the house.

"Can he sleep with me?" Noelle plunked onto her bottom on the floor. The puppy tumbled over to her, and she giggled as she petted him.

"No, he's going to sleep in a crate."

"Why? He won't like a cage. It's like jail. That's mean." Sadie's big eyes shifted to Gracie, imploring her to intervene.

"Actually, dogs feel safe when they have their own comfy little den." She tried to reassure the girl. "We'll cover it with a blanket and put a dog bed inside. He'll love it."

Trent crouched down to pet the puppy. "I have it all set up in the living room. Should we go show him?"

He scooped up the dog, and the girls scrambled to the gate. Gracie closed it behind them. Trent set the pup near the crate. The tiny dog took a leap into the fluffy bed inside, then promptly curled up on it for a nap.

"See?" Trent pointed to the crate. "He likes it."

"It does look cozy." Sadie got on her hands and knees to peek inside. Then she petted the little fellow. He let out a contented sigh. "He's sleepy."

"It's been a busy couple of days for him." Gracie glanced around the room. She'd have to get used to taking the dog out regularly and puppy-proofing the place. She'd always loved pets, so it wouldn't be a chore.

"Why don't we let him sleep, and you girls can select a name for him."

"I'll get a bowl for our papers." Emma strode to the kitchen.

"Are you going to add a name to the bowl?" Trent took a seat on the couch and sprawled his legs out. He looked content. But tired. He ran his hand over his short beard.

"Me?" Gracie shook her head, taking a seat on the chair

kitty-corner to him. "No. He's your dog. You guys should name him."

"You'll be taking care of him, too," he said. "Throw a name in."

"No, really, I'll leave it to the girls."

Emma had returned and held the bowl up. "Do you want to add any more names?"

"I've thought of another." Sadie unfolded her legs and stood.

"Wait, how many do we have?" Trent frowned. "I think we need to narrow it down to one each."

"Only one?" Noelle practically wailed. She made her way over to the couch and climbed up to sit next to him. "But I have lots of names. Lots of good ones."

"Just one." He kissed the side of her head. "That way it's fair."

Emma sighed. "Well, that changes things. Let's get all of the names out and pick our favorites."

After much debate, the girls placed their three selections in the bowl, and Trent wrote down his choice, too.

Gracie held the bowl up high with one hand and reached in with the other. She handed the paper to Trent.

"His name is Digger." Trent's eyes crinkled in the corners. "Who chose that one?"

Sadie raised her hand, her eyes sparkling.

"It's a good name." Emma went over and hugged her.

"Thanks, Em." Sadie gave her a shy smile.

"Diggie, Diggie, Digger!" Noelle ran over and hugged Sadie then Emma. Emma whispered something to them both.

"Thanks, Uncle Trent." They ran over and hugged him.

"Thank Gracie." His face had turned red. "It was her idea."

The girls hugged her and thanked her, too.

Later, back at her apartment, Gracie couldn't stop thinking about what a great day it had been. The best Easter she could remember. Next year the girls would most likely be back in DC with their father. Trent would be fine on his own. Nobody would need her anymore.

He'd told her the horses were his life, and he didn't have room for more.

And she kept conveniently forgetting her own situation. Wasn't she supposed to be taking care of her future? Yet, here she was, enjoying Trent's company far too much.

God, help me get my heart right. Help me rely on You. I'm getting in too deep with Trent's makeshift family, and I'll be the one left alone and sad when it's over.

She took her time going up the staircase and letting herself into her empty apartment. She shouldn't want more. But she did. And she had no idea if she was falling into old, bad habits or was simply enjoying the life she'd been given. Either way, she needed to do a better job protecting her heart.

Chapter Nine

"Is this job becoming too much for you? With the girls and the puppy?"

Trent blinked twice. Cade had requested a meeting this morning—odd for a Wednesday—and they were sitting in the office at the stables. Since Easter, the past three weeks had been a blur of potty training the dog, helping Sadie and Emma prepare for an upcoming school performance, managing the stables and enjoying homemade meals cooked by Gracie.

It had been pure domestic bliss, which in itself added stress. Trent had never really experienced family life. Sure, he'd had his mother, but he'd been alone a lot as a kid.

His work ethic had never been questioned, though. What had he done wrong?

"No. This job could never be too much for me." Trent maintained eye contact with Cade, sitting across from him. "Why do you ask?"

Cade leaned back in the chair. "I stopped by last week after hours and noticed some trash—takeout wrappers—next to one of the stalls. Yesterday, I did a walk-through, and one of the locals' lockers was wide open. That's not how we run things, and I'm surprised you let it happen."

Trent's mind went blank, then whirred back to life. "I'll talk to Jim and Elijah about the trash, and I'll do a thorough inspection every night from now on." It would mean bringing the girls over before bed, but it couldn't be helped.

"I don't want you having to bring your nieces over. I didn't hire you to work twenty-four hours a day. I'm just concerned about things slipping through the cracks that never used to be an issue."

Trent swiped a notepad and pen from the drawer and began jotting notes. "Did you happen to know whose locker was open?"

"Yes. Colin Densing's."

Colin. He'd been the one who'd claimed someone had dumped manure in his horse's stall. And now his locker was open?

"Hmm. I'll look into it. I'll talk to him when he gets here this afternoon." Trent drew his eyebrows together and met Cade's gaze. "We've had a few strange incidents over the past couple of months. I don't know if they're related. If I set up a couple of security cameras in the main aisle, would you have a problem with that?"

"I don't want our boarders feeling like they're being surveilled all the time." Cade didn't seem enthused with the idea.

"I don't, either, but the horses are my main concern. You and I both know small details can become big issues. This is about safety."

Cade considered for a moment. "I suppose we could install two—one near the A-Team's tack room and the other near the locals' tack room. And if nothing shows up, we can turn them off."

"I'll call the security company to set up an appointment to get them installed."

Cade asked when the far pasture would be ready for the A-Team, then they discussed the weather—another storm was supposed to blow in over the weekend—and ranch matters until Cade stood to leave. Trent walked him out of the office.

"Moulten Stables is my number one priority," Trent said. "I don't want you worrying about it. I've got it under control."

Cade hesitated, then nodded. "If it's too much, let me know. I can hire extra help while your nieces live here."

"It's not too much. I don't need extra help. And I'll talk to the teens tonight—remind them of the rules." They said goodbye and Cade left.

His chest burned with mortification. From the sounds of it, his boss was losing faith in him. He'd prided himself on running a tight ship, but cracks had appeared, and Cade rightly held him responsible.

Trent immediately returned to the office and grabbed the notepad. He needed to get a firm grip on what was happening here before he left each evening. His reputation was at stake.

As he inspected each stall, his mind kept flying to the past. To his mother coming home from work late and poring over the bills. To wanting to make life easier for her and not knowing how. To never getting to spend much time together, since she'd worked seven days a week between her two jobs. To the arrangement she'd made when he was twelve. Trent had helped a local rancher in his seventies every afternoon with his horses.

The rancher, Junior, had made strict rules about the stables and horses. His instructions and training had been exactly what Trent had needed. It had given him a purpose—to take care of three horses. He'd watered them, fed them, cleaned up after them and occasionally ridden them.

And he'd gotten his first taste of accomplishment. He'd known caring for horses was the life for him.

Trent couldn't blow it now.

And here he'd thought he'd been doing a pretty good job

of raising the girls and managing the stables. Guess he'd been wrong.

Either he could do his job well or have a personal life. The two couldn't coexist.

As he took inventory of the tack room, Gracie's smiling face came to mind. He liked being with her. More than liked it. He'd been growing close to her. They talked a little longer each night after eating supper with the girls. He trusted the advice she gave him about his nieces. Plus, he liked when she made a point to praise him in front of them. A neglected part of him craved the attention.

But was the extra time with her each night ruining his career?

He couldn't risk that happening.

Something had to give, and it wouldn't be his job. He'd better work harder at all aspects of his life. A temporary family arrangement wouldn't make him lose sight of what was important—his career. He needed to ice over the warm feeling he got whenever he was with Gracie before he lost it all.

"How did the book report go?" Gracie held the door open to Dippity Doo Ice Cream that afternoon after picking up Emma and Sadie. Noelle raced to the counter, and they followed her.

"It went great!" Emma's face glowed. "My stomach was all twisted up before the teacher called on me, but once I stood at the front of the class, I was fine. I told everyone how funny and weird the book was. And get this. Lindsey told me that one of the boys started making fun of my book at recess, but Braeden told him he thought the book sounded cool and for him to shut up."

"See?" Gracie held out her palm for a high five. Emma slapped it. "I knew you'd be great."

"Thanks, Gracie." Emma gave her a hug. "You know, Braeden isn't so bad."

"He sure isn't." Inwardly, she chuckled. The girl clearly had a crush on the kid. Gracie didn't blame her. He seemed nice. And the fact that he'd defended her at recess? A keeper for sure. "What kind of ice cream are we getting? We need to celebrate."

"What are we celebrating?" Sadie stared up at the menu on the wall behind the counter.

"Emma's book report. And surviving winter." She sure was thankful the sun had been shining all week.

"I love celebrating." Noelle clasped her hands. "Can we get a chocolate ice cream for Digger?"

"No, he can't have chocolate." Gracie had gone over the rules regarding Digger about seventeen thousand times with the child, but she couldn't always remember. "It could make him very sick."

"I don't want Diggie to be sick." Noelle's shoulders slumped.

"Besides, the ice cream will melt. We have treats for him at home. You can give him one of his special doggie cookies when we get back, okay?"

Her face cleared and she nodded.

The teenager behind the counter took their orders—four chocolate soft-serve ice cream cones.

"We're celebrating!" Noelle said to the teen when she handed her a cone.

"How nice! What's the occasion?" The girl had a sweet smile.

"We're celebrating winter being over," Sadie replied. Gracie almost clapped her hand to her chest she was so proud that Sadie was the one to speak up. She'd been coming out of her shell more lately. She'd even made a friend in her class who loved to read, too.

"That's something to celebrate for sure." The teen finished their order and Gracie paid for the cones. "You should go to the park. That's what I would do on such a nice day."

"Thank you!" the girls chimed, and then they left the building and got into Gracie's car.

"Can we go to the park?" Noelle asked, furiously trying to keep up with the drips sliding down her cone.

"Yeah, please?" Emma asked.

Gracie set her cone in a cupholder, knowing it was going to melt everywhere, and started the car. It was a nice day. They could spare a few minutes before heading home.

"Yes. We absolutely need to take advantage of the sunshine and go to the gazebo in the park to eat our ice cream." She pulled onto the road, and minutes later, they arrived at the park.

She reached for her purse, trying to keep her cone steady, as the girls tumbled out of the car. She'd better text Trent about their detour. Not that she was worried he'd be upset or anything. Just as a matter of principle.

Ice cream dripped between her fingers. She dabbed it with napkins as best she could and strolled toward the gazebo. The girls had raced ahead and were already sitting at a picnic table. The text would have to wait until she finished eating this melting disaster.

Trent would get a kick out of this scene. Too bad he wasn't with them. She wasn't sure how he'd become so important to her so quickly. She'd been eating supper with him and the girls every weeknight, and the simple act of him asking about her day made her feel like part of the family.

She'd been getting to know him better, too. She'd learned more about his life growing up as the only child of a single mom and how thankful he'd been to get a brother when his mom remarried a few months before he'd graduated from high school. Gracie, in turn, had told him about her lonely childhood and how she'd made peace with the fact that her parents weren't involved in her life.

Gracie cared about him. And she was teetering on the edge of more than caring. Every time she brushed past him, she sucked in a breath and wished they were a couple.

Her phone rang, and she grimaced at the half-eaten cone before tossing it in the trash and finding her phone with her nonsticky hand. The screen displayed Lydia, one of her roommates from Idaho. "Hello?"

"Hey, Gracie." Lydia sounded as upbeat as she always did. The two of them still texted now and then, but they hadn't had a phone conversation since Gracie had moved. Hearing her voice transported Gracie back to when they'd worked and lived together. She felt like a completely different person, and it had only been a few months. "I have a question for you."

"What is it?" Gracie watched the girls eat the last bites of their cones.

"Three of us are heading to the Bahamas on a cruise in July. We were wondering if you'd want to be our fourth?"

The Bahamas. A cruise. She pictured turquoise water, days lounging by the pool, relaxing and laughing with girl-friends. It sounded amazing.

But she glanced around the picnic table at the darling girls in her care, and regret washed over her.

Lydia continued, "I'll email you the itinerary. We found a great deal. Super cheap. Think it over and get back to me by next Friday, okay?"

"I don't think I'll be able to go." She hated turning down the opportunity, but Trent and the girls needed her too much for her to take off an entire week.

"Think it over. That's all I ask." Lydia always advised

her to take her time and not rush a decision. Gracie appreciated that about her.

"I will, but the answer is most likely going to be no."

They caught up for a few minutes before ending the call. She slipped the phone into her purse, found the hand sanitizer in there and wiped her hands free of the sticky ice cream. Then she turned back to the girls.

"Can we swing?" Emma pointed to the playground.

She couldn't deny them the pleasure on such a warm day. "Go ahead."

The trio ran off, laughing all the way, and she slowly followed them. What if she decided to go on the cruise?

Who would take care of the girls and Digger during the day? The puppy was finally in a good routine and having fewer accidents. And what about Trent? Gracie would miss him, miss their suppers together. No. A cruise didn't fit into her life at the moment.

Her phone rang again. My, she was popular today. This time it was Trent. Her heartbeat pounded as she answered.

"Where are you?" He sounded mad. She hadn't heard the accusation in his tone in a while.

"At the park, why?"

"You're supposed to call or text me when you take the girls somewhere." Boy, he was huffy.

"I was going to—"

"But you didn't."

Irritation bubbled up. "We've only been gone twenty minutes. You don't even come home for another hour and a half."

"That's not the point. You promised to tell me when you do things like this."

What did he mean "like this"? Like what? Having a fun after-school treat? Encouraging his nieces to get some vitamin D in the great outdoors? She'd thought he'd gotten over his lack of trust in her, but obviously she'd been wrong. "It won't happen again."

"That's what you said last time."

"Last time? It only happened one time. What exactly are you accusing me of? Kidnapping? Neglect?"

"I just want you to keep your word."

"I do keep my word. I don't appreciate being treated like a criminal."

"We'll talk later."

"I think we've said enough. I will text you with my every move from here on out."

"Don't be dramatic."

"I'm not the one being dramatic."

"I've got to go." And the call ended.

What was that all about? Yes, she technically should have let him know they'd taken a detour to get ice cream and play on the playground, but it wasn't something she'd planned. And her sticky fingers had prevented her from following through with texting him. Then Lydia had distracted her...

She marched in the direction of the swings. Trent should have given her the benefit of the doubt. She'd proven she was reliable and trustworthy. She couldn't count the number of times she'd texted him and called him since she'd started babysitting. With each step, her anger grew.

Lydia's call came to mind. Maybe she *should* consider going on the cruise. She was a single woman, not a wife, not a mother. This was a temporary job—it would be over before she knew it—and then what?

She halted. Oh, no. A pit grew in her stomach.

She'd done it again. She'd claimed a role that didn't belong to her. With her ex, she'd wanted to get married, and he hadn't. She'd moved in, telling herself he needed time.

Taken on the role of his wife, but he hadn't taken on the role of her husband. And it had cost her.

Here she was again—wanting this to be real. Pretending it was real. Romanticizing her days with Trent and the girls.

Trent wasn't her husband. The girls weren't her children. She was the nanny. That was it.

Slowly, she made her way to the bench near the playground and took a seat. Wasn't she supposed to be putting her own needs first? Taking care of herself instead of relying on a man?

Her ex-boyfriend had not appreciated her. And she hadn't been able to rely on him for the important things. And, no, picking up takeout on Friday nights didn't count.

Trent wasn't even a boyfriend. He was her boss.

And yet she knew herself well enough that she'd agree to be his girlfriend if he asked.

But he hadn't asked. He wouldn't, either. He'd been honest with her about his priorities and the fact that the horses and his job would always come first.

The only one who wasn't being honest was her. Once more, she was lying to herself—pouring everything into the girls and Trent and wanting a future with them that would never come true.

With her ex, she'd settled for a house built on sand. And that house had crumbled, leaving her with nothing but a broken heart.

She wanted more from Trent, and she wasn't going to get it.

She was the nanny for three beautiful, special girls. She loved her job. But she'd best keep in mind that's what it was—a job. She checked her email. Lydia had sent her the information about the cruise.

If she really wanted to, she could take the week off. She wasn't going to—she wanted to save her money. But no one found her indispensable. If she began believing she was, she'd only end up disillusioned like before. She wasn't settling for less again.

As soon as he ended the call, Trent had regrets.

He'd taken out his frustration on Gracie, and she wasn't to blame for his bad mood. Yes, she was supposed to let him know when she took the girls somewhere, but she'd been diligent about notifying him until today. One visit to the park—on a gorgeous day like this—wasn't worth arguing about.

Trent saddled up Sarge and headed down the forest trail. Usually riding around and checking the property relaxed him. Today, though, it only keyed him up more.

After Cade had left this morning, Trent had called the security company. They couldn't get out to install the cameras for two weeks. He didn't like having to wait, not when his boss was questioning his abilities. But he didn't have much choice in the matter.

He'd spent the rest of the day inspecting every inch of the stables. Everything appeared as it should.

How could he fix what he didn't know was broken?

He'd been waiting for the teens to load up the horses to take to rodeo practice when he realized Gracie's car hadn't turned down his driveway. It was his habit to watch for it every afternoon—not to check up on her or anything, but because it made him feel better knowing the girls were home. And today, when he hadn't seen it, he'd jumped to conclusions.

He wasn't great with women. Wasn't sure what to say. Except with Gracie. They'd been spending so much time together, he found it easy to be with her. Made him want to spend even more time with her.

Shaking his head, he urged Sarge into a trot. Not two

hours ago, he'd told himself he couldn't do his job well *and* have a girlfriend. So why was he thinking about Gracie now?

He was her boss. The girls needed her. If he pursued her and they broke up, she'd quit. The girls would suffer. That was a risk he couldn't take.

Besides, Gracie would want someone who'd hang out with her in the evening and on weekends. If it wasn't for his nieces, he'd be spending evenings and weekends overseeing the stables, the way he'd done before they'd moved in. The way he should be doing now.

What he really needed was to get Gracie off his mind.

After Trent finished the rounds, he put Sarge back out to pasture with the A-Team.

Jim arrived, and Trent filled him in on Cade's concerns. After the teens returned from practice and tended to their horses, he gathered them all and explained the standards of the stables and that he expected them to be extra diligent about picking up their trash, putting away equipment and locking their belongings each night. Once that lecture was complete, he motioned for Elijah to follow him to the office.

"Am I in trouble?" Elijah asked as Trent closed the door behind them.

"No."

The kid's face cleared.

"Have a seat." Trent sat behind the desk and leaned forward. "Have you noticed anything going on with Colin Densing?"

"Colin?" He frowned. "No, why?"

"There have been a few incidents with his stall and locker, and I figure you're around him more than I am."

"Colin's next-level neat. We all tease him about it. He takes good care of Opie and everything, really. Did you know he's the second-best tie-down roper on the team?"

"I heard he's doing well this year. And that's what I thought about him taking good care of his things." Trent sighed, staring off to the side. "I'm not sure what's going on, but I need you to let me know if you notice anything not quite right. Been a few strange things."

"Strange?" Elijah stared down at his lap a moment.

"Yeah. Like him leaving out trash or forgetting to lock up his tack."

"Hmm…maybe…" He shook his head as if the thought didn't add up.

"What?"

"Nothing. It's just that he and Tori used to be a thing. I thought he was over her, but maybe I was wrong."

Trent hadn't known that. Could the kid have a broken heart? It might be making him forgetful. Would explain a lot, if that were the case. "Thanks for letting me know. Just keep an eye out for me, will you?"

"Sure thing, Mr. Lloyd."

"How is Tori, by the way?"

"Good. She's on her way over." Elijah got to his feet.

"You can go now." As Elijah left, Trent went to the window. Gracie's car was in the driveway across the road. His gut clenched.

He needed to apologize. To make things right. But not in front of the girls. He'd better find a babysitter so he could talk to Gracie in private. He pulled out his phone and called Christy Moulten. After she assured him she'd love to spend a few hours with the girls after supper, he drove home.

As soon as he walked through the door, Digger raced to him. He crouched and scratched behind the puppy's big ears. "How are you today? Full of energy from the looks of it." Then he straightened and prepared himself for an upset Gracie. What if she refused to talk to him later?

"Uncle Trent!" Noelle launched herself into his arms. "We got ice cream and went to the playground!"

"You did?" He glanced over at Gracie, standing at the stove with her back to him. Didn't shock him that she wasn't asking him how his day was. What did surprise him was the fact that he missed her smile so much. He picked up Noelle and carried her over to the table.

Emma was cutting construction paper into strips and had a glue stick within reach. Sadie got out of her chair and came over to give him a hug.

"Hey, Sadie-girl. Did you have a good day?"

"I did. The sun made me happy."

"Made me happy, too." He set Noelle down and turned to Emma. "How did the book report go?" She'd rehearsed it in front of him and her sisters twice this week and done a great job.

"So good!" She briefly looked up with a content expression. "Almost everyone wants to read it."

"That's great." As the girls presented their homework folders with papers to sign, Trent kept an eye on Gracie. He noted the exact moment she left the stove to go to the mudroom. "Excuse me a minute."

He followed her. "Gracie?"

"Hmm?" She wouldn't look at him.

"About earlier."

"Yeah?"

"I'd like to talk to you. In private."

That got her attention. Her blue eyes were full of hurt. "Why?"

"I want to clear the air." He brought his hand to the back of his neck. Why did he feel so hot all of a sudden?

She shifted her jaw. "Why? So you can fire me?"

"No! What? No." He supposed he had that coming. "Can I come to your apartment?"

"When?"

"Give me an hour and I'll be over, okay? I have to drop off the girls at Christy's first. She's babysitting for me."

"I suppose." Then she called out goodbye to the girls and left.

He wondered if he'd made a bigger mess of things than he realized. And he was no longer certain he wanted a life with either his job or Gracie. He wanted both.

Chapter Ten

He was probably going to lecture her. Maybe he'd changed his mind about firing her. Gracie powdered her nose and ran a pink lip gloss over her lips. *Yeah, right. And who would take my place?* Frankly, he had no one else to watch the girls if he terminated her employment.

But that didn't change the fact that she wasn't looking forward to whatever he had to say. Didn't need to hear about being irresponsible or not keeping her word. It made her feel less than. And she'd felt that way enough over the years.

A knock on her door made her sigh. She gave her reflection one last glance and hurried down the hall to let in Trent.

He seemed taller, bigger in her doorway. He'd showered and changed into nice jeans and a button-down shirt. As he entered, she caught a whiff of soap and leather. It didn't affect her. Okay, maybe it did. A little.

"Have a seat." She extended her arm toward the couch. He folded his tall frame onto it and held one of the throw pillows like he wasn't sure what to do with it before setting it aside.

Gracie sat in the rocking chair, tucking one leg under her bottom and facing him. Although the silence was unbearable, she refused to be the one to break it. He wanted this meeting. Let him do the talking.

"I'm sorry I chewed you out earlier." His gaze slid her way.

"Why did you?" If they were having this conversation, they might as well get everything out in the open.

"I didn't see your car come up the drive."

"What do you mean? You watch for it?" Was he spying on her?

"I'm not stalking you or anything. I just feel better knowing when the girls get home." His face was growing red.

"What do you think is going to happen if they're not at home?" She couldn't quite keep the irritation out of her voice.

He was looking everywhere but at her. "I don't know. I just like to know where they are."

She studied him. He still wasn't meeting her eyes. And she realized he wasn't as strong and put-together as he appeared.

"Are you worried something will happen to them when they're with me?" she asked.

"No." His gaze snapped to hers. He was telling the truth. "I know they're in good hands."

"Then why were you so upset earlier?"

"Like I said, I didn't see your car..." His expression fell. "Cade and I had a meeting this morning. He brought a few things to my attention regarding the stables, and it threw me off. I think I know everything going on at work, but I missed those."

"And when you didn't see my car, you thought maybe you were missing things with me and the girls, too." She didn't have the heart to be angry with him. Disappointed, yes. She appreciated that he was willing to be honest, even if it did sting.

"Yeah, I—" he rubbed the back of his neck "—I'm used to being in control. And now I'm not."

Did he think he could hold everything together on his own?

"None of us are," she said quietly. "Not really."

"That's not true." The words chased each other. "Before the girls arrived, I could inspect the stables whenever I wanted. I made the rounds at closing time, made sure everything was the way it was supposed to be. I could be there all weekend. And now I can't be there as much, and things are slipping through the cracks."

"Did you talk to your staff about it?"

"Yeah."

"Do you trust them?"

"Yes, I do. But…"

"But what?"

He shrugged. "They don't care about it the way I do. They don't have the same experience. They aren't responsible for the horses the way I am."

Gracie moved her chin down as she blinked rapidly. Now she understood.

"And you think I don't care about the girls the way you do. That I'm not responsible for them the way you are."

"I didn't say that." His jaw tightened. "But it's a fact that you *aren't* responsible for my nieces the same way I am."

He had a point. He was acting as their guardian.

"I know, but I do care about them. And I feel responsible for them. As responsible as a mom would. They're important to me, Trent."

He sighed, looking at the ceiling briefly. "I know. That's why I'm sorry about the way I talked to you earlier. I was in a bad mood, and I took it out on you."

Gracie couldn't believe he was apologizing. "Well, I should have texted you. I'm not used to checking in with anyone, but I meant to. The ice cream dripped all over my fingers, and then I got a call and forgot."

"I'm sorry I made such a big deal about it. I'm not used to checking in with anyone, either. It's hard trying to keep track of three kids on top of my job. I worry all the time."

"I didn't realize…" A few more things clicked into place. "Knowing where we are takes some of the stress off you, doesn't it? One less thing to worry about."

"Exactly." He nodded. She couldn't look away if she tried. Did this guy have any idea how handsome he was?

"I thought you were having me check in with you because you didn't trust me."

"That's not it, Gracie. I know you have the girls' best interests in mind. You care about them. If I'm being honest, it's not just them I worry about."

"I know. You're concerned about the horses. And you need to give them your full attention, which is hard to do when you're worried about where the girls are."

His lips pursed together as he shook his head. "That's true, but that's not what I was about to say."

She wasn't sure where he was going with this.

"It gives me peace of mind to know where you are, too."

Her muscles froze as her memories rewound. All those years of coming home to an empty house while her parents worked. The weekends of running around with friends, her folks not caring where she was or who she was with. Later, devoting her life to a boyfriend as negligent to her as her parents had been.

For the past two years, she'd been trying to dampen her need for someone to care about her. And now, Trent was saying the very words she'd longed to hear most of her life. What did it mean?

"Why?" she asked. "Why would you care?"

He blew out a breath. "I don't know. I just don't like the thought of anything bad happening to you. If you were in trouble and needed help, I wouldn't have the first clue how to get to you."

She rose and moved to sit next to him on the couch. "What kind of trouble?"

"What if your car broke down on one of the country roads?" He shifted to face her. "Or some fool got dazzled by your pretty blue eyes and decided to harass you?"

Pretty blue eyes? Spring blossoms bloomed in her heart. He wanted to protect her?

"I do have pepper spray." She couldn't believe how happy— giddy, really—his words were making her.

"It's something, I guess." He shook his head dismissively. "But it won't do you much good if— I just…"

She held her breath, waiting for him to continue. When he didn't, she prompted him. "You just what?"

His eyes flitted with questions and quandaries. His knee began bouncing. Then he met her gaze. "I like you. I don't want anything to happen to you."

He liked her. Romantic bubbles floated all around her.

"I like you, too."

"As a boss? A friend?" His tone fished for more.

"Yes, as a boss. And as a friend." Dare she admit the truth? "And more."

"How much more?" His tone lowered and his eyes shimmered.

"I don't know. I guess that depends on you."

"I don't have much to give." His face fell.

"We don't need to rush this." She covered his hand with hers. "I'm not ready for a big commitment. I'm not even ready for a boyfriend."

"I don't know if I'm capable of giving you what you want."

His eyes were telling a different story, though. They were saying, *Yeah, I could commit to you. I can see a future with you.*

"What now?" she whispered.

"How about…this?" He moved closer to her, tentatively placed his hand behind her neck and pulled her to him. Then he lowered his mouth to hers, and she closed her eyes, not sure what to expect but anticipating it dearly.

The instant his lips pressed against hers, she was overcome with a sense of belonging, of being needed, of needing this man in her life. A lingering taste of peppermint teased her senses, and she couldn't keep up with all of the sensations his kiss brought on. The muscles flexing in his broad shoulders. The way he held her as if he wanted to crush her to him but feared he'd break her. The murmur escaping her lips as she kissed him back.

For a fleeting moment all she could think was, *This is what I've always wanted.*

But Trent ended the kiss, and all thoughts flew away, leaving her vulnerable and unsure.

"Gracie." The word was a promise, a warning, a plea.

She searched his eyes, not knowing what to say or do.

"This isn't smart," he said.

"I know." Dumbest thing she'd done in a long time.

"It crept up on me. You're easy to talk to, and I like coming home and sharing about my day and hearing about yours. And I think it messed me up."

"Me, too. I like all that, too. And I'm definitely messed up."

"You're not messed up." His eyes softened as he tucked her hair behind her ear.

"Then you're not, either."

"If we're doing this, we've got to take it slow."

"Are we doing this?" She let her hand curve over his shoulder, down his arm, liking the feel of his muscles.

"I can't let anything jeopardize our arrangement. The girls need you."

"I know. I worry about that, too."

"I wish this wasn't messy. I wish it was straightforward."

Gracie wished the same. "We'll have to be careful. We'll take it slow."

He smiled. "My thoughts exactly."

"Are you sure?" She cocked her head to the side.

"About what?"

"About me?"

He took her hands in his and stared into her eyes. "I'm not sure about anything. But I know how you make me feel. I know I like being with you. I know I have a hard time staying away."

Music to her ears.

He straightened. "I'd better pick up the girls."

She walked him to the door, and he turned to her one more time. Tenderly ran his fingertips down her temple to her cheek. Then he kissed her other cheek and let himself out.

After she closed the door, she pressed her back to it and tried to control her pounding heart.

What had just happened? Trent had kissed her? Admitted he worried about her? Liked being with her?

But he'd been hesitant about a relationship, too. And for mostly the same reasons as she was.

Three little girls needed her and their uncle to be mature and to put their needs first. What if Trent realized she wasn't worth the trouble? What if he broke things off with her?

Too many what-ifs for one night.

She crossed over to the couch and hugged one of the throw pillows to her chest. *God, I don't know if I'm ready for this. I'm not supposed to date anyone right now, am I? What if I'm setting myself up for heartbreak again? I want to do Your will. Help me know what to do!*

Trent's face came back to mind. His eyes, so full of appreciation for her. The gentleness in his touch. The need for her in his kiss.

She'd be careful. Take it slow. If he, like her ex, decided she wasn't worth the hassle, she'd be devastated. She already admired Trent more than any man she'd met. Maybe their kiss, their agreement to take it slow, had been a mistake.

Or maybe it was the start of a whole new chapter in her life. She didn't know. And she was afraid to find out.

Two weeks later, Trent rode the perimeter of the summer pasture and admitted to himself he had *not* been taking it slow. The sun was shining, and the temperatures had risen to the sixties—a nice change from the snow flurries a week prior. Hard to believe the end of May had arrived. In two days the girls would be out of school for the summer. He and Jim had moved the horses to the summer pasture. They'd checked every inch of the fence, ordered extra troughs for watering the horses and had been spring cleaning around the outbuildings.

Possibilities filled the air—from the rodeo team finishing their season to the routine he'd gotten into each evening with Gracie and the girls. She'd been staying later each night, and after supper they'd play a board game or read books with the girls. Then the five of them would take Digger for a walk across the road to the stables.

He was falling for Gracie French, and he wasn't sure what to do about it.

A part of him warned it wouldn't last. Couldn't last. But the other part yelled to enjoy it while it did.

After checking the fence, he rode the trails along the back of the property, keeping an eye out for any areas that needed to be addressed. A branch had fallen in the pathway, and there were a few deep grooves a little gravel would fix.

A few hours later, he'd filled the grooves, and the teens

poured into the building with their noisy laughter. There had been three more minor incidents since Trent had reminded them of the rules. A missing bridle, a soda spill left overnight in Opie's stall and a mix-up with hay. He didn't like it, but there wasn't much he could do. The security company had come out, but the cameras had been defective, so they'd had to reschedule for next week.

Elijah stopped in the office doorway. With his chin to his chest, he didn't seem his usual optimistic self.

"Something wrong?" Trent motioned for him to come inside.

"No." His face said yes, though.

"I hope you know you can tell me if you've got something on your mind."

"I'm fine." He didn't sound fine.

"Here you go." He handed him his chore list. "You sure everything's all right?"

One shoulder lifted in a sad shrug. "Tori's mad at me. She says I spend all my time at the stables and not enough with her."

Trent was taken aback. He'd been down that road before. Several times.

"And I told her it was my job. That it was important." The kid's voice grew bolder, and he met Trent's gaze. "I like taking care of the horses, you know?"

"I do know." Trent nodded. "You do a good job here, too. Not everyone has the work ethic you have, and I hope you recognize that it's a gift, not something to be ashamed of."

His face had fallen again. "Thanks, Mr. Lloyd. I'm going to work on my list." He plodded away.

Trent chewed on the conversation. He hadn't realized his problem with women applied to other guys, too. He wasn't the only one who suffered for prioritizing horses and his job.

Poor kid.

A few minutes later, Samantha Fowler stood in the doorway and knocked. He waved her inside.

"I hear you came close to placing in barrel racing last weekend," he said as she took a seat across from him. She wore worry like Noelle wore joy. Odd, since Samantha tended to exude self-assurance.

"I did, but I'm pretty sure it's because two of the best girls had the flu and couldn't compete." A small smile lifted her lips, but her clasped hands revealed white knuckles. "I don't want to bother you—"

"You're not bothering me."

She relaxed a notch. "Good. It's just... I've been hearing rumors about this weekend."

He straightened, leaning forward. "What rumors?"

"I don't know. Friday's the last day of school, and competitions are over, so we'll all be here to take care of the horses." Her shoulders climbed to her ears as she stared at him through wide eyes. "And I heard something about Colin being mad about Tori dating Elijah and trying to get him fired."

That would explain a lot. Trent tucked that comment away. "Did you hear anything specific?"

"No. Not really. But I appreciate what Mr. Moulten's doing here for us on the rodeo team, and I don't want our horses kicked out just because someone's jealous."

A pit grew in his stomach. Samantha was on the verge of tears. He needed answers, but he also had to treat her gently.

"You did the right thing coming here to tell me. I'll keep an extra eye out for things this weekend. And if you hear anything more or remember something, no matter how small, talk to me or Jim, okay?"

She nodded and stood.

"Oh, and Samantha?"

She turned to him.

"We like having the rodeo team boarding your horses here. We always root for y'all."

Her smile dispersed the cloud of worry surrounding her. "Thanks, Mr. Lloyd. I'll let you know if I hear anything."

"Good." He watched her leave, then considered what she'd told him. Rumors about Colin and Tori and Elijah and jealousy. That Colin might have a problem with Elijah dating his ex.

For some reason, it wasn't quite adding up.

He didn't know why. But he did know he had to figure out how he could keep an eagle eye on this place all weekend. He wasn't letting anything happen to the stables, the grounds and especially not to the horses.

Not on his watch.

He had too much at stake.

"What are we going to do first?" Emma ran to Gracie Friday night and gave her a hug. After supper, Gracie had gone back to her apartment and loaded her car with everything she'd gathered for their sleepover. "I can't believe we're done with school for the summer!"

"First? I'm going to put all my stuff in the living room. Oh, and I brought snacks." Gracie held up two bags from the supermarket. Her large duffel dangled from her other arm. "I need to grab my pillow and blanket from the car, too."

"I'll get it." Trent, with his sleeves rolled up and wearing jeans, took the duffel from her. "Thanks again for doing this."

"I'm happy to. It's way past time the girls and I had a sleepover. Girls' night!"

Digger raced from the direction of the living room, and he wiped out in his haste to greet her. Emma took the grocery bags, and Gracie picked up the wiggly pup. "How's my Digger-Poo? I've only been gone a few hours. You couldn't have missed me that much."

"He does." Sadie came into the kitchen and gave her a hug. Digger wiggled and licked Gracie's face. She set the puppy down, and he continued to circle ecstatically in front of her.

"Gracie!" Noelle ran full-throttle and wrapped her arms around her legs. "You're here! I can't wait for girls' night!"

On his way to the living room, Trent looked back over his shoulder and let out a loud groan. "I'm not painting my nails, so don't even think about asking."

"But I brought four shades of pink." Gracie tried to sound offended but couldn't help grinning. "You have to at least try them."

"No," he called from the other room.

She rubbed her hands together. "We'll convince him to try my special shea butter hand lotion."

Emma giggled. Sadie looked confused. And Noelle hopped up and down in front of her, yelling, "I love hand lotion!"

Trent returned. "Do you all want to check the stables with me? Digger can come, too."

"Yes!" Noelle ran to the mudroom.

"Wear your sneakers, okay?" Emma followed behind her. Sadie scurried off to join them, leaving Trent alone with Gracie.

He came over and kissed her cheek. Discreetly. The twinkle in his eyes made her heart flutter. "Thanks for agreeing to this."

"Of course." She wanted to take his hand, to reach up on her tiptoes and kiss him, to have him wrap her in his arms. But they were taking it slow. And they'd agreed not to be affectionate in front of the girls. Too confusing for everyone.

"After we check the stables, I'll stay with you guys until around ten. I don't know if I'm going to stay there all night or come back."

"Whatever makes the most sense to you." She wanted to reassure him but wasn't quite sure how. "It's good that you're taking the rumors seriously."

"I hope nothing comes of it."

"I hope so, too."

The girls argued their way back to the kitchen. "He *has* to wear a harness, Noelle. He'll choke to death if he doesn't." Emma yanked the leash from Noelle's hand.

"That's mine!" Noelle lunged for the leash.

Sadie appeared with Digger's blue harness.

Time to intervene. Gracie turned to Noelle. "Honey, would you go to my car? In the back seat, you'll see a pillow. Can you bring it in for me?"

With tears forming in her eyes, she nodded. Then she spun on her heel to leave. Gracie looked at Sadie. "Can you go help her? Maybe bring my blanket inside?"

Sadie flashed a smile and handed Emma the harness. Then she took off after Noelle.

"Digger won't choke to death without a harness, you know." Gracie crouched to Emma's level.

"I know, but Noelle can't handle his leash, and I hate seeing him gag. I thought he was going to throw up the other night, he was choking so hard."

"I agree he needs his harness. Just try not to be too hard on your sister." She straightened. "Why don't you get his harness on? Then we'll all head over together."

Fifteen minutes later, after several skirmishes over who got to hold the leash, Gracie and the girls stood outside the stables and waited for Trent to type in the alarm code and unlock the door. Then they went inside.

"I love the smell in here." Gracie turned to Trent as the girls raced ahead on their merry way to see their favorite horses. He held Digger's leash.

"Manure?"

"No!" She playfully slapped his arm. "The straw, the hay, the dirt. It's cozy."

"Cozy, huh?" He handed her the leash. "I've always thought so, but I know I'm not like most people."

"I guess I'm not, either." She let Digger sniff around the stalls as they headed down the aisle toward the locals' horses. "Do you really think Colin would do something to the stables?"

"I don't want to think he would." Trent was checking each lock on the stalls as his eyes took in everything around him. "But I need to make sure nothing happens."

"How would he even get in?" She tightened the leash when Digger got a little too interested in a bucket.

"He couldn't. We change the alarm code at least once a week, and only Cade, Jim, Elijah and I have keys."

"It would be difficult to sneak in through the pasture." The way the property was laid out, the only way someone without a key could access the grounds was by sneaking through a pasture. But they'd have to climb a fence, make it through the ditch, walk across acres of pastures, and they still wouldn't be able to get into the locked buildings.

"Not impossible, though." They emerged into the hall. "We have cameras at the entrance. If anyone decides to come by uninvited, we'll know who they are. I just wish the indoor ones could have been installed."

"And I wish you didn't have to deal with this." She bent to pick up the puppy. He was panting and smiling at the same time. "Let's not wear you out too much, Digs. We have a full night of fun ahead of us."

Trent checked the lockers and made sure all of the equipment was where it was supposed to be. When he was satisfied, Gracie gathered the girls, and they all went back to the farmhouse.

"Should we start with a snack? Manicures? Board game? What?" Gracie asked after everyone had washed their hands and settled in the living room.

"Snacks. I want to practice how to French braid." Emma looked at her sisters, practically daring them with her eyes to challenge her.

"I want gummy worms." Noelle clasped her hands to her chest. "And I'll brush your hair, Gracie."

"You will?" She blew the girl a kiss. "That's sweet of you. So, gummy worms. French braids. What do you think, Sadie?"

The girl turned to Trent. "Uncle Trent, are you staying here all night?"

"Um..." He gave Gracie a look that screamed, *How do I answer?*

She took pity on him and addressed Sadie. "He's going to be checking on the horses. So he might stay in the stables if he gets sleepy."

He nodded his thanks.

"But you'll be lonely." She walked over to him and sat on his lap. "And what if there's a snake over there? Or a robber comes?"

"I'm not going to be lonely." He hugged her to him. "And I'm not afraid of snakes. We don't get too many robbers in these parts. I'll be fine."

"I don't like it." She shook her head.

"There's no need to worry about me, Sadie. I've been taking care of myself for a long, long time. Just have fun tonight, okay?"

The child didn't look convinced, so Gracie made a lassoing motion toward the kitchen. "Come on, let's get our snacks."

An hour later, Emma was happily chattering away as she practiced French braiding Sadie's hair. Gracie sat cross-legged on the floor as Noelle brushed hers, and Digger was curled into a ball on her lap. They'd turned on the animated version of *Beauty and the Beast*. Sadie seemed enthralled with it. Emma wasn't paying attention to the television, and neither was Noelle. A bowl of chips, a plate of brownies and bags of candy spilled out on the coffee table. Trent had excused himself a few minutes ago to grab a sweatshirt.

"I'm taking off." He entered the living room. They all turned to him. "Girls, listen to Gracie. Do what she says. I'll be right across the road."

Emma finished the braid and wrapped an elastic around the end. "Will we have breakfast together in the morning?"

"Eggs, bacon, hash browns and toast." He kept his gaze locked on Emma's. She gave him an approving nod.

"Can we go to Annie's Bakery and get doughnuts, too?" Noelle's words ended in a giant yawn.

"I'm sure we can make a trip to get doughnuts."

Gracie turned her attention to Sadie, who was quiet. As usual.

"What do you want for breakfast, Sadie?" Gracie asked.

"I don't want you to go, Uncle Trent." The words were soft, yet each one came through loud and clear.

He went over to her and picked her up. She let her cheek fall against his shoulder.

"It won't be for long. When you wake up, we'll have breakfast and doughnuts. Don't worry."

Gracie couldn't help thinking he was a natural with the kids. Patient, understanding, strict but not too strict.

"Now, don't eat too much candy, okay?" He kissed Sadie's head and set her back down.

"Bye, Uncle Trent!" Noelle ran into his arms, and he hauled her up and kissed her cheek. Then Emma came over and hugged him.

Gracie lifted the sleeping puppy off her lap and followed him to the mudroom. "Be careful. I can't guarantee I'll be awake when you get back."

He chuckled. "Thanks for staying with them."

"I'm happy to be here."

"Keep an eye on Sadie. She's worried." His fingers found hers and tangled together.

"She'll be okay."

With a nod, he opened the door and slipped out into the night.

That meant phase two of the evening could commence. She went back to the living room. "Who's ready for nail polish?"

"Me!" Noelle scrambled to her. Emma followed. And Sadie wrapped herself tightly in her blanket with her eyes fixed on the television screen.

Around midnight, Trent got antsy. He'd been sitting on hay bales in an empty stall near the middle of the barn. So far, nothing—and he meant nothing—out of the ordinary had happened. And that was a good thing. Was all this a waste of time?

For the past hour, his mind had been on a loop—a figure-eight loop. It started with the stables and the horses and what could possibly go wrong here this weekend. Then it circled to Gracie and how much he enjoyed being with her and how he wanted to make a relationship work with her at some point.

They were taking it slow. Tell that to his galloping heart.

A popping sound in the distance jolted him upright. What was that? He stilled, training his ears for any other noises. Nothing.

Should he stay in place or investigate? His nerve endings sizzled. He had too much nervous energy to stay.

He quietly padded down the hall, exited the building and searched the surrounding area for movement. The popping sound had probably come from the woods. The stars and moon provided enough light that he didn't need a flashlight. His eyes adjusted to the dark quickly, and his arms swung as he took long strides. If someone was out there, he doubted he'd find them. But he'd at least do a circuit around the outbuildings and front pastures.

After ten minutes of fast-paced walking and seeing nothing, he rounded back to the lane, his gaze automatically lasering to the stables.

A light was on. Inside.

All night, he'd kept the lights off. He broke into a sprint. If anything happened to the horses, he'd never forgive himself. Why had he left them alone? He'd been warned.

He should have stayed there.

His heels ached in his cowboy boots, he could barely catch his breath, and with each pounding jog closer, his anxiety spiraled out of control. Finally, he reached one of the double doors.

That's when he heard the scream.

A split second passed before he launched himself forward. Turning the corner, his worst nightmare was coming true. One of the horses was rearing up in the aisle. And Sadie was right below its hooves.

The horse was terrified. And a huge, frightened animal could kill her.

"Sadie, get to the side," he yelled.

She immediately flattened herself to the wall as the horse came down. It raced ahead and turned the corner to the hall, where it had nowhere to go. Trent waved for Sadie to stay where she was, then switched to his soothing voice and slowly approached the panting horse.

Opie. The one with the white cross on its forehead. Colin's horse. The frightened beast's ears were radaring, and a whistling noise streamed from his nostrils.

"Hey, there, Opie. What scared you, huh?" He kept his tone low and nonthreatening. The horse was well trained and calmed relatively quickly. Trent waited until it came to him, and then he stroked its neck and whispered sweet nothings into his ear. It didn't take long for him to lead the horse back to its stall and get him settled. He locked the stall and hurried to Sadie, still flattened against the wall and shaking. Tears streamed down her pale face.

He swept her into his arms and rubbed her back as she gripped her arms around him tightly. "Sadie-girl, are you okay?"

He felt her nod, and she clung to him even tighter.

"What were you doing here?" What exactly had happened? Sadie couldn't have opened Opie's stall—she didn't have the key. So who had opened it?

"I heard a loud noise, and I looked out my window and saw you outside, and I got scared that a bad man was going to get you, so I ran over. The lights went on before I got to the door, and I thought you were in here."

"How did you get in?" He'd locked the front door hours earlier, and the alarms had been on all night.

"It was open."

He continued to rub her back as he carried her to the office. He had a million things to do, but he couldn't formulate what he should face first. He couldn't leave Sadie, that was for sure. Inside the office, he sat down with her on his lap.

"I need you to tell me everything you remember, okay?" He looked into her scared little face and could barely tamp down the anger and fear festering inside him. Who would do this? Who would put his precious Sadie in this kind of danger?

If it was Colin…but why would Colin hurt his own horse? It didn't make sense.

"When I got inside, I saw Opie's door open. I heard a slap and someone ran away." She began crying again.

He clenched his teeth together but kept his touch gentle as he stroked Sadie's hair while she cried.

"Did you see who it was?"

She shook her head.

"Boy? Girl? Tall?"

"I-I-I do-o-o-n't know."

"Okay, okay. It's okay. I'm going to make a few calls and get you back home."

"I don't want to leave you!" There went her death grip around his neck again.

Lord, I need some help here. I could have lost her! I need to find out who did this, but I can't solve anything with Sadie clinging to me.

He held her for a few more minutes and pulled out his phone. The first call he made was to Cade. "Sorry to wake you, but there's been a serious incident at the stables."

"What's wrong? What happened?" Cade sounded deadly concerned.

Trent explained what he knew. "I've got to get Sadie home so I can investigate. Figure out who got in here, how they did it and more importantly, why."

"Call Jim and Elijah. They both have keys. Whoever hurt that horse? I'm pressing charges."

"I will right now."

"I'm calling the police."

"Good."

"I'm on my way. Whatever's going on, we need to put an end to it. Now."

The line went dead, and Trent shifted his jaw again and again. Then he called Jim. And Elijah. The kid sounded like he'd woken from a dead sleep. He told him they had an emergency at the stables and to get over there. He put his phone on the desktop and looked down at Sadie, shivering on his lap.

"As soon as Mr. Moulten or the police arrive, I'm taking you back home."

"I want Gracie." The words were so puny and heartfelt, they crushed him.

Gracie.

Where had she been during all of this? How had she let Sadie out of her sight long enough to come over here? Why hadn't she been checking on the girl?

His body throbbed with pent-up frustration. He'd have a long talk with Gracie later. For now, he had enough to worry about. It was going to be a long night.

Chapter Eleven

The sound of the door opening, then closing, woke Gracie. She squinted at her phone. Just after one in the morning. Sitting up from where she'd fallen asleep on the couch, she figured Trent must have come home to get a few hours of sleep. She couldn't wait to see his face and, hopefully, cheer him up. He'd been tired and worried all week.

The atmosphere changed, though, when he carried Sadie into the living room.

"What's going on?" Gracie scrambled to her feet and rushed to him with her arms out to take Sadie, but he held the girl tightly.

"You tell me."

"What do you mean?" She mentally tried on a dozen scenarios, but none of them added up.

"Why weren't you watching her?" The words sounded more like a snake hissing than human speech.

"I was." She had been, right? "The girls went to bed around eleven. Noelle fell asleep before then, so I carried her to her room. But Sadie and Emma went to bed at the same time."

"Then how did you miss the fact that Sadie came downstairs and *ran all the way to the stables by herself*?"

The fury sparking from his eyes chastened her. Her pulse grew weak, and her thoughts instantly went to condemnation mode. She'd messed up. She wasn't sure how, but she had.

"Sadie went to the stables? By herself?" No wonder he was furious. She gently rubbed Sadie's back and tried to meet her eyes, but the girl's head was buried in his shoulder. "Sadie, are you okay?"

Silent sobs shook the girl. What had happened to frighten her so?

Gracie stared up at Trent. "May I?"

He gave her a cold nod. She took Sadie from him and carried her over to the couch. Set her on her lap and rocked her side to side. "I'm here. You're safe."

"She wasn't safe," Trent said in a low tone. "I have to get back to talk to the police."

"The police?" She furrowed her eyebrows together. "Why? What in the world happened?"

"You and I will have a long talk when I get back." He pointed to her. "A horse almost trampled Sadie, and this entire situation is unacceptable." With that, he pivoted and left the room.

A horse? How could a horse have come near the girl? They were all locked in their stalls at night, except for the ones left out in the pasture.

The only thing she knew for sure was that Trent blamed her for whatever had happened.

Now Gracie felt like crying. Instead, she murmured comforting words to Sadie and continued to rock her as she cried. It took several minutes for her to calm down.

Gracie stroked her hair and kept her arms around her. "Why don't I make us hot cocoa? Will that help?"

Sadie hiccupped as she nodded. Gracie set her on the couch, then got up and went to the kitchen. She didn't want to grill the poor thing, but she did need a better understanding of what had happened. After she heated up milk and poured it into mugs with hot cocoa mix, Gracie took the mugs over to the couch and handed one to Sadie.

"Why don't you tell me what happened?" She gave the girl the most understanding, sympathetic expression she could muster.

Sadie let out a sad sigh as her shoulders slumped. "A firework noise woke me up, and I jumped out of bed and looked out the window. I saw Uncle Trent near the pasture, and I thought a bad man was going to get him."

"I'm sorry, honey, that must have been scary."

"It was." She sipped her cocoa with wobbling lips. "I normally like to look out the window because I can see the stars and the pastures across the road, but I got scared this time."

"I like seeing the stars, too." She took a drink of her cocoa, trying to make it safe for Sadie to continue. "And I don't blame you for being scared. Did you see someone besides your uncle?"

"No. Just him. Everyone was asleep, so I put on my shoes and ran over there."

"I wish you hadn't done that, but it was brave of you."

Sadie's sad eyes grew watery again. She took another drink.

"What happened when you crossed the road?" Gracie figured she must have gone to the pastures if a horse had reared up.

"A light went on inside. I thought Uncle Trent was back, and it made me feel so much better. I ran into the stables, but I saw Opie's stall open, and the horse came out, and there was a slap and someone ran away and he got up on his back legs like this—" she curled her arms up in the air "—and Uncle Trent told me to get against the wall."

The girl set her mug down, dropped her forehead into her hands and cried again.

Gracie put her arm around her. Sadie twisted and clung to

her for quite a while. "Shh…it's okay. You're with me now. It's going to be all right."

After a few moments, she stopped crying.

"Why did you think your uncle needed you to help him?"

She grew very still and didn't respond.

"He's an adult." She smoothed the girl's hair from her forehead. "He can take care of himself."

"Mommy died. And Daddy's gone. I don't want to lose Uncle Trent, too." The final words were barely a whisper.

"Oh, honey." Gracie rocked her again, kissing the top of her head. "I'm so sorry. You've had too many losses. I understand. You love him. We want to protect the ones we love."

She nodded, nestling into her embrace. "I do love him, and I thought I'd never see him again."

"Your heart was in the right place, but next time you're worried, you have to get an adult involved. You're too important to us. We can't lose you, either."

"What do you mean?" She shifted slightly to look up at Gracie.

"You running off into the night—if you'd twisted your ankle or gotten lost—we would have had no way to know where you were."

"I didn't think about that."

"And I realize your mommy died, but most grown-ups don't die until they're old. Really old. Like gray-hair-and-wrinkles old." She tried to inject levity into her tone. "Your daddy is on a mission, and he *will* return for you. You haven't lost him. And your uncle has been taking care of horses and stables his whole life. So if there had been danger, he would have known exactly what to do."

Sadie glanced up at her. "Are you mad at me?"

"No, honey. I'm not. I could never get mad at you for having a big heart. But you can't run off by yourself ever again."

"Am I in trouble?"

"That's not up to me to decide. I figure you've had enough of a scare tonight to learn your lesson, but your uncle will make that decision."

"I'm sorry, Gracie."

She kissed the top of her head again. "You're forgiven."

"Just like that?"

"Of course." She smiled. "Remember? That's how Jesus does it. We repent and God forgives us. He loves us so much, there's nothing we could do that He wouldn't forgive. Sometimes we have consequences, though."

"What are those?"

"When you don't return your library book on time, you have to pay a fee. When we don't take out Digger right away, he has an accident, and we have to clean up a mess. When you break something of Emma's, you have to replace it."

"Oh, I see. What do you think my consequence will be?"

"I'm not sure."

Sadie soon fell asleep in her arms, leaving Gracie's mind churning with all that had gone on. Now that she knew Sadie's side of the story, she had questions for Trent. They'd grown so close lately, surely he wouldn't blame her for everything that had happened tonight. But he *had* been furious.

It had been a rough night for all of them. She hoped they caught whomever was responsible. She never wanted Sadie to be this upset again.

As soon as Elijah and Jim arrived, Trent brought them into the office and explained what had happened. In the parking lot, Cade was talking to the police. It would be hours before the sun rose, and Trent had a feeling it would be hours before his heart stopped racing, too.

"Talk about a bad day." Elijah couldn't stop shaking his head. "First, Tori broke up with me and now this?"

Ever since taking Sadie back home, Trent had been inspecting the crime scene more fully, and he'd found a blue furry key ring with two keys sitting in the straw just inside Opie's stall door. On a hunch, he'd tested to see if one of the keys unlocked the stall. It did. And the other one unlocked the front door. Both were copies of the master keys.

"Have either of you seen this before?" He held up the key ring.

Elijah held out his hand to take it, and he grew pale as he flipped it over. "It's Tori's. I've seen it in her purse. I needed a piece of gum, and it was there."

Tori's? That shed new light on the evening. She and Colin had dated. Then she and Elijah had dated. And now, apparently, they'd broken up.

"Why would she have keys to the front door and a copy of the master key for all the stalls?" Trent glared at Elijah.

Jim crossed his arms over his chest and shook his head.

"She didn't. She couldn't have." Elijah's eyebrows dipped into a V so low, it gave Trent a headache just looking at him.

"If you're correct, and this is hers, then she did. And I think she must have been the one who came back here tonight and let out Opie."

Cade and two officers entered the office. Trent took the key ring from Elijah and handed it to the police. After a lengthy interrogation, the police dispatched another officer to go to Tori's house for questioning. In the meantime, Trent checked on all the horses again.

More flashing lights appeared outside, and soon Tori and her mother came into the office to hash out what had happened with the police and Cade.

"I wasn't here," Tori said defiantly, glaring at Elijah. "I was hanging out with Jenna."

"That's not what Jenna and her parents said." One of the officers stood in a wide-legged stance. Then he held up the key ring. "This has been identified as yours."

She blinked a few times and blanched.

"Were you lying to me?" Tori's mom turned to her with an incredulous tone. "You weren't at Jenna's?"

Tori shrugged.

"Answer me. Were you here tonight or not?"

"We have security cameras," Cade said calmly. "We'll know if you're telling the truth or not."

Tori hesitated. "You don't know how humiliating it was when Colin broke up with me. I am so sick and tired of the rodeo team. I figured I'd show him that I belonged, too."

Trent narrowed his eyes in confusion. Where was she going with this?

"Even when I was here with Elijah, Colin acted like I didn't exist."

Elijah stepped forward, and the pain in his expression actually hurt Trent. "You only dated me to get back at him?"

She must have known how bad this made her look. "You and I were never going to work, Elijah. You know that."

"Why?"

It was Cade's turn to step forward. "You were the one who left trash outside Colin's stall, yes?"

She didn't respond.

"And dumped manure in there, too?"

Her gaze shifted down to her feet.

"And when none of that worked, you stole Elijah's keys and had copies made. Watched him type in the code and noted any changes." Cade's voice was flat and terrifying.

"My niece could have been killed." Trent expanded his

chest and glowered at the girl. "What would ever possess you to let a horse out of a stall in a locked barn?"

At that, her stony mask crumbled. "I didn't know she would be here. And I was going to open the doors to let Opie run outside!"

"How is that better?" Trent asked, glad he'd gotten her to confess. "That horse could have been injured or attacked by a wild animal. It was terrified."

"I'm sorry!" She burst into tears and turned into her mother's arms.

"Why tonight? Why now?" Cade asked.

"Elijah said indoor cameras were being installed next week. I couldn't wait any longer. Plus, Colin has a big competition coming up."

"You really wanted to ruin his life, didn't you?" Trent asked quietly. A sense of horror had rippled through him at her reasoning. She gave him the creeps.

"I wanted him back." The words were clear and truthful.

The police began asking more questions. Another thirty minutes passed before Tori, her mother and the police officers left, leaving Trent with Cade, Elijah and Jim.

Cade came up to Elijah and clamped one hand on his shoulder. "Don't blame yourself. This wasn't your fault."

"But it *was* my fault." The kid's face was ashen. "I can't believe she was only dating me to get back at Colin. And I let her in here… I didn't know she'd make a copy of my key. And I didn't think to hide the keypad when I punched in the code. I'm dumb. I'm an idiot. You're firing me, aren't you? I deserve it."

"No, Elijah. You're not fired, and you're not dumb." Cade patted his shoulder twice. "We all make mistakes. Trust me, I've made some big ones. You're a good employee. We wouldn't have hired you, otherwise. Now, stop beating yourself up. Go home. Get some sleep. Take the weekend off, okay? We've got it covered."

"Thanks, Mr. Moulten." He sniffed. Then, with his head hanging low enough for his chin to hit his chest, he came over to Trent. "I'm really sorry, Mr. Lloyd. I'm sorry about your niece. And I'm sorry for being so stupid. And—"

"I appreciate your apology, Elijah." Trent gave him an understanding nod. "We'll see you back here on Monday."

"Come on. I'll walk you out." Jim put his arm around Elijah's shoulders, and they left.

Cade strode over to the desk and took a seat. The bags under his eyes had grown heavy. "What a night."

"Tell me about it."

"How are you holding up?"

"I'm okay," Trent lied. "I'm just glad we found out who was behind everything. It won't happen again."

Cade knocked on the desk twice, bringing him back to the present. "I'm sorry I blamed you for the stuff going on here. I didn't realize we had a stalker on our hands."

"Don't apologize. I'm responsible for this place. I should have known what she was up to. I'm the one who's sorry. I've got to tell you, though, I've never dealt with anything like this."

"I haven't, either." Cade screwed up his face in confusion. "You couldn't have known, though. She was sneaky."

"I shouldn't have allowed her to be here when Elijah was closing up."

"Half the rodeo team stays until he's done."

"Yeah, well, I should have had new master keys made."

"Because?" Cade let the question linger.

"Because it was obvious something was going on, and I should have known about it. I could have prevented it!" His voice grew louder, and he had to physically restrain himself from slapping his palm on the desk.

"Listen, man, you're tired. You're being way too hard on yourself. It's been a tough couple of months for you. I don't want to see you back here until Monday. Ty and I will take care of everything this weekend. Get some rest. That's an order." He stood and set his cowboy hat on his head. "Now, let's get out of here."

Trent grabbed his hat and gave the office a final glance before following Cade outside. They locked up, said goodbye and got in their trucks.

A few minutes later, Trent entered his mudroom and took his time washing his hands under the hot water. His stomach was tying itself into knots and unraveling them over and over. His hands shook as he dried them off.

When he got into the living room, he halted. Sadie was sleeping on Gracie's lap, and they looked so much alike, they could have been mother and daughter.

He didn't have the luxury of sappy thoughts right now. Gracie's eyes were wide open, but she didn't say a thing. He marched over and carefully took Sadie in his arms. Then he carried her to her room and tucked her into bed. Sadie's eyelids fluttered. "Uncle Trent?"

"I'm here, sweetheart."

She closed her eyes and smiled. "Good. If you're here, everything will be all right."

The words pinged his heart. But he didn't have time to dwell on them, just kissed her forehead and quietly made his way downstairs. Gracie was primly sitting on the couch with her hands clasped in her lap and her big blue eyes questioning him. He checked the dog crate. Digger was sleeping.

He collapsed into the chair adjacent to her and ran his hand across his forehead. Then he took a deep breath.

"What happened?" Her soft tone spiked his anger.

"What didn't happen?" He shook his head. "Tori, Elijah's girlfriend, was on some loopy vendetta against one of our boarders—her ex-boyfriend. She stole Elijah's keys, made copies, broke in tonight, and I honestly don't even understand what she thought the outcome would be. She claimed she wanted her ex back. But I don't see how that could happen if she set his horse loose and got him kicked out of the stables permanently. The whole thing is messed up."

"What?" Her nose scrunched in shock. He didn't blame her. Confusing didn't begin to describe the events of the night.

"Yeah. And she was so selfish, she didn't care that her actions almost caused Sadie to be injured or killed. I shudder to think of what could have happened. The horse could have gotten hurt or lost. And Colin didn't do anything to deserve his name getting dragged through muck or for his horse to be mistreated."

"Oh, Sadie. Little Sadie…" Gracie's voice broke.

"Yes. And little Sadie." He glared at her. "Where were you? What were you doing? You're honestly telling me you didn't hear her leave?"

"I didn't. I should have." She seemed to be searching for answers and not finding them.

"I trusted you to take care of her." He knew he wasn't being fair. But nothing about this night was fair. He and Gracie were the adults. They were the ones who protected the girls and the horses. And she'd let him down. She'd let Sadie down.

"I know. I feel terrible."

"Terrible doesn't cut it. She ran out into the night—" His breath seemed to pause in his lungs. "When I think about her running across the road in the dark and following Tori into the stables…"

When he thought about the horse rearing up and her terrified little face…

"I know. It's so horrible. I couldn't bear it if anything happened to her." Tears started falling to her cheeks.

"Then why did you let it happen?"

She blinked rapidly. "I didn't know, Trent. I would have never let her go if I had known. What do you think happened? That she came over and told me she was saving her uncle from a bad man and I said, 'Go on and have fun.' You know me better than that. I was sleeping and had no idea she wasn't up in her bed."

She was right. He knew she was right. And yet the fear and adrenaline from the night were pushing out words he had no business saying.

"It cannot happen again." He leaned forward, shaking his head. "Promise me. I cannot have that happen again."

She straightened and tilted her chin slightly. "What exactly am I promising?"

"That you won't put my girls in danger again."

"I didn't put them in danger." The words were clear and without emotion. "I stayed right here. Played with them. Put them to bed. Said their prayers. Took the puppy out. Slept on your couch."

"Maybe you slept too deeply."

"Maybe you're not being fair."

He wanted to shout out all of the things he'd held in earlier when Cade and the police were questioning Tori. About how selfish Tori had been and how her thoughtless actions could have seriously hurt so many people. But it hadn't been his place.

"I'm going home." She moved stiffly, picking up the nail

polish bottles lined up on the coffee table and carrying them to her duffel. "I thought…"

Danger hovered in the air. One more word and he'd ruin everything. "What?"

"I thought we'd moved past it."

"What are you talking about?"

"Who I was before I moved back. What you really think of me. I don't think you'll ever give me the benefit of the doubt. And I don't want to get close to you anymore."

"Guess what? You won't be the first woman who doesn't want to get close to me. No woman wants what I have to offer—not even my own mother did—and I don't care. I'm over it." He regretted raising his voice at the end. He hadn't planned on saying those words. Hadn't allowed himself to think them.

"Yeah, well, my mom wasn't close to me, either, and you don't see me chasing you away. You don't see me thinking the worst of you. I don't deserve that. I don't." Her voice wobbled, and a fresh batch of tears slipped down her cheeks. She scrambled around, tossing items in the duffel. Then she marched to the kitchen.

Dread and realization hit him. He'd said too much. Been too harsh. He followed behind her. "I'm not chasing you away."

She glanced over her shoulder. "You are."

"Fine. Call it what you want. You won't see things my way."

"Because your way demands perfection. And perfection doesn't exist. Keep looking for it, buddy. Make yourself miserable."

Perfection? What was she talking about?

She opened the door and left.

He wanted to keep arguing. Wanted to burn up the difficult emotions churning inside.

But he watched in silence as she got in her vehicle, started it up and reversed out of the drive. Then he closed the door and went back to the kitchen. As he started a pot of coffee, he realized his hands were shaking. He gripped the edge of the countertop with his arms wide and let his head drop. He closed his eyes, trying to calm the turbulence racing through his body, and one thought kept shouting at him.

She's right. You're wrong. She's right. You're wrong. She's right...

He'd just ruined the best thing that had ever happened to him. And he couldn't bring himself to do a thing about it.

Chapter Twelve

"I did it again." Gracie sat on her couch with a soft throw over her lap, her earbuds in and a mug of coffee in her hand. It had been several hours since she'd left Trent's place, and they'd been hard hours. No sleep. Lots of what-ifs. No closure. She'd finally called Brooke when she was reasonably sure she wouldn't wake her.

"That's not true." Brooke's voice soothed her.

"It is. I think I'm only attracted to emotionally unavailable men who don't really need or want me."

"Don't say that."

"Why not? It's the truth."

"That does it. I'm coming over. I'll have Dean watch the girls."

"You don't have to—"

"Yes, I do. I'll be there soon." The line went dead.

Gratitude surged, but it wasn't enough to cover the pain of Trent's words. She'd been fooling herself. Seeing what she'd wanted to see. Hearing what she'd wanted to hear. Living in her own fantasy bubble. Just like before.

But this time it felt even worse. Because she'd told herself—promised herself—she wouldn't do it again. Wouldn't get all tangled up in a man's life if she wasn't important to him.

Trent's accusations didn't even bother her as much as the fact that he'd proven, deep down, he didn't trust her. All the nights of hanging out together with the girls, the flirty glances, the way they discussed mundane things like if Noelle needed new sneakers—all the trips to the stables where they often touched hands. All were an illusion of the feeling of belonging she'd missed her entire life.

And she'd better not even think about their one kiss right here in her apartment.

She brought the mug to her lips. *No thinking about that. Think about anything but that.*

Was Sadie okay? She'd been so upset and shaky and traumatized last night, it was all Gracie could do not to drive over there and verify for herself the girl was all right. She still didn't feel like she'd been given the whole story. Yes, she had the details, but some of the whys were missing.

The biggest one? Why did Trent blame her for everything that had gone wrong?

She wasn't the one who'd broken into the stables and let a horse loose. She wasn't the one who'd put Sadie's life in danger. Yes, she should have woken up, but Sadie wasn't in the habit of running across the road in the middle of the night.

Her thoughts continued to circle back until she'd been over the same scenarios too many times to count. When a knock on the door interrupted them, she hoped beyond hope that Trent would be on the other side, ready to apologize. But she knew he wouldn't be there.

She opened the door and tried not to show her disappointment at seeing Brooke. Her best friend surged inside and gave her a long heartfelt hug. The disappointment quickly shifted to gratitude. Someone was in her corner.

They settled in the living room with more coffee.

"Rough night, huh?" Brooke sipped her coffee.

"The roughest."

"The way you two left things—do you still have a job?"

"Yeah. I guess." Gracie hadn't thought that far ahead. She'd been reliving the night, rehashing their argument. She hadn't considered her future. "I mean he could fire me."

"Who would he have watch the girls, though?" Brooke shook her head. "I can't think of anyone available."

"I don't want him to find someone else. I'll be their nanny. I just won't be making supper or staying over and hanging out with them once he comes home."

"But you love those walks to the stables." Brooke seemed to be taking this as hard as she was, and for some reason, it comforted her.

"They were built on a lie."

"A lie? What do you mean?"

"I believed Trent was truly interested in me. We talked about taking it slow, getting to know each other. I mean... he kissed me. Once. But I misread the situation."

"Okay."

"Now I know how he really feels. Deep down, he thinks I'm unreliable and untrustworthy."

"I'm not defending him." Brooke set her mug on the end table and put her hands up. "But I'm sure he was upset about the night. We all know how much the stables mean to him. And to have someone deliberately jeopardizing the horses— well, I'm sure that must have hit him hard."

"Yeah, so hard that he blamed me for it all."

"I'm sorry. That wasn't fair of him."

"I know. I just want a guy who sees the best in me. Who can handle me making a mistake. Who won't yell at me but will wrap me in his arms and tell me I did my best."

"I want you to have that guy, too." Brooke shook her head, her curls settling over her shoulders. "I want to go over there and tell him how stupid he's being."

"Me, too." They met each other's eyes and grinned.

Another knock on the door revived the earlier hope. She got up and went to the door. Reagan stood there.

"Brooke said you had a rough night. I figured I'd pop over. Hope that's okay."

Their thoughtfulness brought tears to the backs of her eyes. "Come in. Of course, it's okay. Thank you. But where's little Elizabeth?"

"Marc's on baby duty. I've barely left the ranch since having her, and I needed a break."

Gracie got Reagan a mug of coffee, and they went over everything that had happened.

"I don't think he distrusts you, Gracie," Reagan said.

"You could have fooled me."

"Seriously, when Marc and I were getting close, there was a big issue between us that neither of us wanted to address."

"That's right. He wanted the building you owned." Gracie had completely forgotten how difficult it had been for Reagan when she and Marc had first met. He'd wanted his mom to expand her bakery in the building Reagan owned, but Reagan had planned on opening her chocolate shop there. They'd ended up swapping spaces.

"I actually walked away from him," Reagan said. "For good. The day he handed me the building permit and told me his mom deserved the building more than I did, I was done. I felt so dismissed and betrayed."

"I hate that for you." Gracie's heart twisted.

"But God worked on his heart, and Marc realized he'd been wrong. He's never dismissed my needs again."

"I don't see that happening with Trent." Everyone had great love stories that worked out so perfectly. That kind of thing didn't happen to her.

"I'm just saying," Reagan said, "I wouldn't be surprised if he apologizes. Even if it takes him a while to get there."

"Full disclosure." Brooke pulled a slight grimace. "I was the one who had to apologize to Dean. I was awful to him when he literally was saving my life. I had a lot of emotional baggage to unpack and deal with before we could admit we loved each other."

"Both of your situations are different." She didn't want to spell out that they were the most amazing women she knew—of course their guys were scared of losing them. She'd yet to meet anyone who found her impossible to live without. "I mean if he apologizes, I'll accept it. But I don't think I trust him anymore. I don't want to go any further with someone I'm not absolutely certain thinks the best of me."

"You shouldn't! You deserve someone who treats you like the amazing person you are." Brooke nodded firmly.

"I agree. You're honest and kind, fun, generous and like a big burst of sunshine whenever I see you." Reagan settled deeper into the corner of the couch. "Have I told you how much I love your apartment? Pink everywhere! I wonder if I could get away with redecorating one of the rooms in pink."

"Elizabeth's." Brooke grunted.

Gracie chuckled. "You should give it a try in the living room. Do it slowly. Add a pillow or a vase. Then keep adding pieces until it's as pink as you want."

"I just might do that." Reagan smiled. "I'm glad you moved here."

"I am, too," Gracie said quietly. And she was. But it was going to be difficult taking care of the girls and avoiding their uncle. Because she was starting to realize she'd gone way beyond the taking-it-slow phase and skipped ahead to *I-actually-love-the-guy.*

She couldn't do it. Couldn't love a man who held her in such low regard.

And yet she was pretty certain she loved him.

Could she be any worse at choosing guys? She doubted she'd be able to get over Trent, either. She'd try, but she'd meant it when she'd said she needed someone who thought the best of her, not the worst.

That man didn't exist.

She might as well face it. She was meant to be alone.

Around noon, Trent sat at the kitchen table and stared out the windows. A beat-up Bible lay open in front of him. He'd been flipping through the pages, reading a verse here and there. Earlier, he'd fallen into a brief, restless sleep, then he'd changed into sweatpants and tried to make sense of his life.

His life made no sense.

None at all.

How had he gone from enjoying his dream job and feeling great about himself to completely failing at the job and feeling like a loser?

And, worse, blaming Gracie and the girls for it all?

He wiped his hand down his cheek as exhaustion weighed on him. He flipped through the pages of the Bible again, not really knowing what he was looking for. He stopped in the book of Matthew and scanned the pages. A bit of text caught his eye. *The parable of the unforgiving servant.* He read through the section and felt sick to his stomach.

"Uncle Trent?" Emma poked his shoulder. He hadn't heard her come down. He gave her his attention and realized Sadie and Noelle stood shoulder to shoulder with her. Noelle held Digger in both arms. His little tongue panted softly.

"Yes?"

"Sadie needs to see Gracie."

"She does?" The words were whisper-thin. He peered at Sadie. He'd talked to her and held her when she'd woken up this morning, tried to make sure she really was okay. But at the moment, she looked pale and tiny standing there in her leggings and blue shirt. Emma must have done her hair. It was smoothed back into an uneven braid.

Sadie nodded, her eyes round with sincerity.

He couldn't see Gracie today. Not after all the things he'd said.

"You'll see her on Monday."

Sadie bowed her head, but he'd caught a glimpse of her pinched face.

"She can't wait that long." Emma put her arm over Sadie's shoulders. "She needs to talk to her now."

"I don't know…"

"We need to go over there." Emma wasn't giving up.

Noelle set the puppy on the floor, ducked around her sisters and climbed up on his lap. "I don't want a horsie to hurt me."

What had the girls told her? He hadn't sat them down and talked to them about what had happened, mainly because he hadn't known what to say. Plus, his mind had been on Gracie. How they'd left things.

"None of you girls need to worry about a horse hurting you. Not like what happened last night, anyhow." The strength returned to his voice. "Someone was in the stables who shouldn't have been there, and she let the horse loose and scared it on purpose. That's why it almost hurt Sadie."

"Who was it?" Emma asked.

"A girl from the high school. Don't worry about it. The horses we board are all well-behaved, and as long as you follow the rules we've gone over, you don't have to worry about getting hurt."

A squeaky noise escaped from Sadie and he frowned.

"I didn't follow the rules." Her voice quivered and tears formed. Why was she still beating herself up? He'd told her it wasn't her fault. "Are you going to send me away?"

"No! Come here, Sadie." He helped Noelle hop off his lap and pulled Sadie close to his side. "I would never send you away. It wasn't your fault the horse was loose. Do I ever want you running out in the night like that again? No. But you're not to blame for any of this, okay?"

She held herself rigid. Great. He hadn't gotten through to her at all.

"Is Gracie still going to be our babysitter?" Emma's eyes conveyed her worry.

"Of course," he said with too much bravado. "Why wouldn't she?"

"Sadie said you were really mad last night. That you were mad at Gracie."

He thought back to what Sadie had heard. He *had* been mad when he'd carried the girl inside and found Gracie on the couch. What had he said? Whatever it was couldn't have been much. He'd left pretty quickly to meet the police.

"It wasn't her fault," Emma said.

"I appreciate you sticking up for her, Em, but—"

"I don't want her to leave." Sadie started crying for real this time, and all he wanted to do was to cover his face with his hands and go back to bed for a decade. "I'm sorry I didn't tell her I was going across the road. Don't be mad at her. Don't make her go away!"

"Uncle Trent, we all talked, and you can ground us or give us extra chores, but we promise we'll be good if you'll just keep Gracie." Emma's composure cracked, and as he looked into her eyes, he saw the toll these past years had taken on her. He could see how strong she'd had to be after their mother died. How brave she'd had to appear when their father announced they were moving to Wyoming for a year without him. And he could see the uncertainty of a nine-year-old girl who'd had too much placed on her shoulders.

In some ways, he saw himself in her eyes, except he'd never had siblings as a kid. Just the burden of trying to get through life without consistent adult supervision.

"Everyone sit down." He waited for Noelle and Emma to take their seats. Sadie slid off his lap and sat in her chair, too. "No one is getting grounded or having extra chores."

"But—" Emma looked stricken.

"No one is getting punished." He tried to be as gentle as possible. "We all make mistakes, and I know Sadie will not do it again. Neither will the two of you, right?"

They all nodded.

"I don't give you rules to make your life miserable. They're to keep you safe. So, I want you to put this behind you and just do what you normally do. Let's enjoy the weekend. We'll go to Dixie B's later for supper, okay?"

Something unspoken traveled between the girls, and Digger came over to Trent and stared up at him, letting out a yip. He picked up the dog and petted him as he sat there waiting for the girls to enlighten him with whatever they still grappled with.

"We need to see Gracie." Emma wasn't letting this go.

"You'll see her at church tomorrow." A panicky feeling came over him. He wasn't ready to talk to Gracie. He'd only make things worse. As if they could get worse.

"We can't wait."

"Why don't you call her?" He set the dog down and patted his pockets for his phone, but it wasn't there.

"We need to *see* her. In person." Emma's tone grew more insistent.

He blew out a breath as his head tipped back. "Look, girls, I'm tired. It was a long night—"

"Please?" Noelle's voice cut through the air.

Shifting his jaw, his gaze went from Noelle to Sadie to Emma and what he saw in their expressions humbled him.

They needed Gracie right now. Each one of them. And probably for different reasons.

"Let me call her. If she's free, I'll take you over there. But before I do anything, I'm taking a shower."

They turned to each other and nodded in unison.

If he had his way, he'd avoid Gracie for...well, for as long as it took to pretend last night hadn't happened. She probably wanted to avoid him, too. He'd been cruel, and he didn't think of himself as a cruel person.

He pushed his chair back and stood. "Why don't you play with Digger while I get cleaned up?"

"We're coloring." Noelle stood, clapping her hands with a happy twinkle in her eyes. "Diggie can sit on my lap."

He wasn't going to argue. He was just glad they were amusing themselves and not crying. He'd made enough people cry over the past twelve hours. And at some point along the way, he'd realized he'd responded all wrong.

His standards weren't realistic at all. They were impossible for anyone to reach. Gracie was right. He demanded perfection. And contrary to his internal beliefs, he was the least perfect of all of them.

He didn't deserve a second chance—not with his job at the stables and not with Gracie.

In some ways, he was the unforgiving servant in the parable he'd read. And he hated that this was who he'd become.

He'd take the girls over to her apartment—if she agreed to it—and he'd stay in the background. Or leave and pick them up later. He wasn't ready to face her disappointment. He wasn't ready to face his own. He'd made too many mistakes, and he couldn't see a way around them.

Chapter Thirteen

Nervous energy rushed through her veins as Gracie fluffed her pink throw pillows. Trent had called earlier and told her the girls needed to see her. He hadn't apologized. Hadn't said much at all. But she'd agreed to have him drop them off, and they'd be here any second.

Why did they need to see her? If she knew them at all, they'd agreed on a plan. Those sweet little girls. She loved them. Maybe too much.

They weren't hers. Would never be hers. But she could love them in the meantime.

As for their uncle? Sadly, as the day wore on, she'd accepted that she did indeed love him. Not as a friend. No, she'd fallen for him in the worst way. Her heart had been breaking since last night, and after Brooke and Reagan had left earlier, she'd spent some time in prayer.

All the things she'd learned back in Idaho, all the things she'd promised herself when moving here—she'd decided to embrace them from here on out.

She wasn't going to be considered inferior in a romantic relationship ever again. No one was allowed to treat her as second best.

God had taken away her sins, and He'd hidden her under the shadow of His wings. The Bible made it clear that He loved her beyond imagination. And when she closed her eyes and thought of God, she always pictured herself running into open arms. Loved. Protected. Cherished.

Maybe getting close to Trent hadn't been a mistake. The experience was allowing her to test her resolve. She still didn't know if she'd pass that particular test or not.

Straightening, she took in her pretty, bright apartment. The life she'd built here revolved around Trent and the girls, but she'd get along fine after they moved back with their dad. And she'd limit her time with Trent. She had friends, a great apartment and, best of all, a spine.

The knock on the door didn't startle her, but she took a moment to inhale deeply and pray. *Lord, please give me discernment with the girls. Help me say what they need to hear. And give me strength and courage to be mature around Trent.*

She opened the door. The girls poured inside, and he stood there in the doorway. She could practically pluck the regrets from him. Something in his eyes sank her spirits.

"I'm stopping at the hardware store." He jerked his thumb behind him. "When I get back, I'm taking the girls over to Christy's for a bit, and I'm hoping you and I can talk."

"We can talk." The old Gracie would have clung to his words, would have built a scenario where he'd beg for forgiveness and tell her he couldn't live without her. But the new-and-improved Gracie was more realistic. She doubted he was capable of offering what she needed at this point in her life.

He nodded, his gaze asking her if she was all right and saying he was sorry she was hurt, but those eyes were also holding back from the heart of the issue. She gave him a tight smile and closed the door. Then she turned to the girls. They were sitting on her couch in a line. Emma on one end, Noelle smooshed next to her and Sadie next to Noelle.

Something was off. None of them fidgeted. They weren't talking and interrupting each other. They weren't even staring off into space.

All three sets of eyes had focused on her.

"What's wrong?" She couldn't help herself; she immediately hugged Sadie and kissed the top of her head. "Are you doing okay, Sadie? I've been worried about you all day."

The girl blinked, and her face cleared slightly. "You have?"

"Of course. You had an awful fright." Then she hugged Noelle and kissed the top of her head before turning to Emma with a hug and a kiss on the top of her head. Finally, she sat in the rocking chair.

"You're not mad at me?" Sadie's voice was so small it hurt to hear it.

"No, silly, why would I be mad?" She gave her an understanding smile, trying to put her at ease.

"Uncle Trent was angry last night. And he yelled at you." Sadie seemed to shrink into herself. "But it was my fault. I'm sorry. I'm sorry I left, and I'm sorry I got you into trouble."

"Oh, honey." Gracie shook her head. "You didn't get me into trouble. Your uncle was upset because he was scared. And people who are scared sometimes come across as angry."

As she spoke, she realized she hadn't added that up about him until now.

"He sounded real mad." Her forehead wrinkled in worry.

"Seeing you in danger frightened him. He loves you—all three of you—" she met the other girls' gazes "—so much. He'd never forgive himself if anything happened to you."

Another realization. Trent was more than capable of love. A real, deep, true love.

Emma cut in. "Are you still going to be our babysitter? We all promise we'll never break the rules again, will we?" She nudged Noelle and gave a warning look to Sadie.

"We promise." Noelle nodded.

"It was my fault. I won't do it again. I'll be good." Sadie sounded and looked like she was being tortured.

"Of course I'm going to be your babysitter," she assured them. But then she remembered Trent coming back to have a talk. "I will be for as long your uncle wants me to be your babysitter. It's his decision. But whatever happens, I love you—all three of you. You're very important to me."

"We love you, too." They all got to their feet and surrounded her in a group hug before settling back on the couch.

"Now, all this business about being good and never breaking the rules?"

They all watched her in suspense.

"I'm glad you want to do the right thing. But sometimes we make mistakes. And when you do, I don't want you worrying about not living up to my expectations or your uncle's. I don't want you to think you have to be good to be loved."

"I don't understand." Emma, in particular, seemed confused.

How could Gracie get through to them? "You go to church and Sunday school. What do you always learn when you're there?"

"Jesus loves us!" Noelle shouted.

"That's right. And does He love us because we're perfect?"

Emma's mouth twisted. "No, He knew we needed a Savior."

"Because we were born sinful," Sadie added.

"That's right. And there's no mistake too big that God won't forgive. It's like that with me and your uncle. We love you. We know you're going to make mistakes sometimes, and we still love you. Just like we make mistakes, too, and you still love us."

The girls asked more questions. Then Gracie handed out cookies, and before she knew it, Trent had returned.

"How did it go?" he asked as the girls headed to the door.

"Great." Emma gave him a satisfied nod.

"Okay, then, we'd better go." He waited for them to leave the apartment before returning to Gracie. "I'll be back in a few minutes."

She nodded and he left. She knew why she had so many problems in the romance department. It had taken years of bad decisions, months of wallowing in her victimhood and a long time living according to new standards to get to where she was today.

And she wasn't going back to the needy, dependent girl she used to be. But Trent…did he know the real reason why women didn't get close to him? Why was he scared? He'd lost a lot—he'd told her about the losses.

His father dying when he was a toddler. In some ways, he'd never gotten his needs met by his mother. It was no wonder he'd turned to his career to create the stability his life lacked.

He was capable of loving deeply. But if he didn't recognize it, what difference would it make?

She'd listen to what he had to say, but she doubted it would be what she wanted to hear.

How could he make this right? How could he tell her what he felt?

Trent sat on Gracie's couch with those pink throw pillows to his left and to his right. He'd dropped off the girls at Christy's place, and they'd been back to their normal selves. Whatever they'd discussed with Gracie must have satisfied them.

Gracie shifted uncomfortably in the chair. Besides the gray circles under her eyes, she looked as beautiful as ever. She wore a lavender T-shirt and jeans. Her hair fell in soft waves over her shoulders. To his surprise, she didn't appear to be angry or even upset. Instead, an air of calm surrounded her.

Maybe that's what kept drawing him to her. She didn't get rattled.

She did have a quizzical expression, though, and he realized he'd better start talking.

"I said things I shouldn't have last night." He ran a finger under the collar of his T-shirt. "I'm sorry."

"Sorry you said them?"

"Yes, of course." He was missing something.

"But not that you thought them."

Context. That's what he'd been missing. "I was upset."

"And blamed everything on me." She didn't sound angry or hurt. He narrowed his eyes, trying to figure out her mood.

"I…" Yes, he had blamed everything on her. "I shouldn't have."

"Who would you blame then?"

He didn't know. Tori. Himself. Elijah. Maybe they were all to blame.

"No one was perfect last night." He let his knees open wider. "I think we all deserve some blame."

"Fair enough." She tilted her head slightly, never taking her eyes off him.

"But I deserve the most." He'd had too much time to think today. And he'd been unable to avoid some tough truths. The Bible passages he'd read had seared into his mind. "Have you ever read the parable in the Bible about the unforgiving servant?"

"He owes his boss a lot of money and begs for mercy. The boss forgives him his debts."

"Yeah, and then he runs off to someone who owes *him* money—a fraction of what he owed his boss—and the guy begs for mercy."

"But he doesn't forgive him his debt."

"Exactly."

The silence in her apartment was interrupted by the sound of a vehicle driving down the street.

"What are you getting at?" she asked.

His throat was closing up. Why was this so hard?

"I'm the unforgiving servant." He pushed out the words.

"What do you mean?"

"Last night, Cade could have fired me. I'd unintentionally put his business in jeopardy. He could have fired Elijah, too. But he showed us grace and gave us the benefit of the doubt."

"Cade seems like a nice guy."

"He is." He tapped his fingers against his thighs. "And I'm not."

She didn't argue. He didn't expect her to.

"He showed us mercy, and instead of doing the same, I lit into you. Accused you."

"You were scared. You needed someone to blame."

"It doesn't make it right."

"No, it doesn't. Maybe you were scared about more than Sadie."

"I was. I feared I'd lose my job."

"More than your job."

"The girls. For sure."

"More than the girls." She'd straightened and was holding herself rigidly. "You and I have been getting close. You've told me about the women you dated. How they made you feel like you had to choose between your job and them."

"But you never made me feel that way." She hadn't, either. It was one of the reasons he was so drawn to her. One of the reasons he loved her.

He loved her. Couldn't deny it anymore. Didn't see the point.

"I never will, either," she said. "Your job is a big part of you. Important. That makes it important to me, too."

"Then what are you saying?" He dared not hope she'd let him off this easy.

"You demand perfection from yourself. And from me. And you're never going to be happy with me."

What? "I'm already happy with you."

She shook her head. "No, you're not."

"Yes, I am."

"Trent." The word acted like a stop sign. "Until you learn to accept that perfection is impossible, you'll fall back into blaming me whenever something bad happens. I don't deserve that. I don't want to have that in the back of my mind. Waiting for the next crisis to come along and get blamed for it."

"I wouldn't—"

"You would." She sounded sad. "So, I'll be leaving each weekday as soon as you come home. We can make it work for the girls' sake. They need me. You need me—for them. And I need them."

"What if I told you I love you?"

"I'd say you'd just be telling me what I want to hear. You don't want to do the emotional work to be my boyfriend."

Was it true? He wanted to refute it. "I do want to be your boyfriend. More than that…eventually. You made me think it's possible for me." The enormity of what he was losing smacked him in the chest. "I like eating supper together and walking over to the stables discussing our days."

"I do, too, Trent. I love it. It's my favorite part of the day. But I can't do that anymore."

"I'll change." He stood, rubbing the back of his neck and having no clue how to change. "I'll be the man you want me to be."

"I don't want you to be anyone but who you are."

"Then what's the problem? I don't get it?"

"You have to love yourself before you can love me." Her eyes pleaded with him to understand. And he didn't. "I'm talking about all of you—your strengths and your flaws. You have to accept yourself, or you'll never truly accept me."

He sat back on the couch, sinking into it. "I don't know how to do that."

"You'll learn."

"What will you be doing during this?" It hit him that she might start dating one of the local cowboys. Fall in love. Get married. The kind of love she was talking about could take years. He might never learn to love himself.

"I'll be right here, Trent. I told you a long time ago, I'm doing things right this time. I'm not in a rush. I might never find a man who will treat me the way I want him to, and I'm making my peace with that."

"I want to be that man, Gracie. I...I love you."

Her smile was so sad it broke his heart. "I know you don't say that to just anyone, and I appreciate it. But I don't think you really do. Not the way you think you do."

Her words anchored in his gut, and his mind spun. This conversation wasn't what he'd expected.

"I guess..." He planted his palms on his thighs and stood. "I guess that's all there is to say."

"I guess so."

Was he imagining the tears glistening in her eyes?

"I'll let myself out." He set his cowboy hat on his head and headed to the door. "You won't change your mind about babysitting?"

To his surprise, she'd followed him. She shook her head. "I won't change my mind."

He turned to face her. "Can I give you a kiss?"

"You'd better not. I… My heart is too wrapped up in you already."

It should have made him feel good. Should have given him a sense of victory. But it didn't.

Because while he knew he loved her, he had no idea of how to prove it to her.

"You're asking the impossible, you know." He ran his finger down her cheek to her chin. "You're the easiest person in the world to love. And me? Impossible."

"With God, all things are possible, Trent." She reached up and kissed his cheek. His gaze lingered on her eyes, and it took all his willpower to open the door and leave.

All the way down the stairs to the parking lot, he bit his lower lip and shook his head. Gracie was right. The way things stood right now, he couldn't be the guy she deserved.

But he was willing to do as she asked. Accept himself. Love himself.

He just didn't know how.

Chapter Fourteen

Trent said goodbye to Jim on his way out of the stables, lifted his face to the sunshine and got into his truck. The past three weeks had been difficult—and so worth it.

At first, not having Gracie around in the evenings had left a void he'd been unsure how to fill. But he'd continued his nightly routine with the girls. After supper, they'd put Digger on a leash and walk over to the stables around closing time. Sadie had developed a shyness around horses that Trent was trying to help her overcome. Starting next week, the girls were all beginning horseback riding lessons. Elijah and Trent would be teaching them.

Elijah had grown quieter since Tori's betrayal. As for Tori, she was getting counseling and doing community service. She'd also been permanently banned from Moulten Stables.

Trent had been trying to help Elijah move on. It wasn't easy, and he suspected it would take time. He understood about personal growth taking time. Shockingly, the horses and stables weren't at the top of his priority list anymore.

He'd taken to opening up his Bible after the girls went to bed. Praying. Sitting with himself instead of turning on the television. It made him feel antsy sometimes. But he'd noticed a difference. When he was home, he wasn't constantly thinking of all the things he needed to do at the stables. He did his work and left it there. And when he was at work, he didn't feel the need to watch the window for the girls and Gracie to arrive home. He focused on his job.

At some point along the way, he'd finally accepted himself. He'd thought back on his childhood, and he felt sorry for all the pressure his mother had been under. She'd had a tough life and had done her best with him. He wished she was still around. He missed her. But he also knew he'd needed more from her. And, in some ways, he'd been working himself around the clock the way she had, but for different reasons.

Starting the truck, he checked his surroundings and backed up. His relationship with the Lord had undergone a shift, too. The need to live up to self-imposed, unrealistic expectations had dropped away as he'd read through the Gospels. Jesus had paid the price for Trent's sins. And Trent wanted to live his life in gratitude for his salvation, not trying to earn something already freely given to him.

Last night, he'd confided in the girls that he was in love with Gracie and needed to convince her to take a chance on him. Those three girls had put their heads together to come up with a plan. Their quick minds terrified him sometimes. But, in this case, he was thankful for their ideas.

He drove home, went inside and released Digger from his crate. He petted the dog and took him outside. Then Trent went upstairs, changed into fresh jeans and a T-shirt, went back downstairs and got everything ready. He'd driven two hours round trip this morning to pick up two-dozen pink roses from a florist, and he'd put together a playlist of romantic music. Now, all he had to do was wait. He perched on a stool at the counter and kept one foot on the ground.

Digger pranced around his legs until he picked the puppy up. "You don't like not being able to see everything, do you?"

He chuckled. "We're a lot alike, you and me. I wish I could see how Gracie's going to take this."

Although they hadn't been spending as much time together, he didn't think she hated him. She still gave him shy glances more often than not. She never kept a smile from him. And she always discussed the girls if he brought one of them up.

But could he convince her he'd changed?

He didn't know.

The sound of her car driving up then stopping made his heartbeat *tap, tap, tap* like a woodpecker in a tree. The mudroom door opened, and the girls were all talking over each other.

"I'm getting out the jump ropes." Emma's voice was as precise as ever.

"No, Em, we said we're going upstairs and writing down all the memories from this year." Sadie's quieter voice had an adamancy about it.

"I want cookies!" Noelle had one volume—ten.

"You have time for all those things," Gracie said, laughing. "Why don't you journal for a while and have a snack? Then you can come down and jump rope. I'll get the cookies ready. You can take them up with you."

They entered the kitchen and spotted him. All three girls ran to him and gave him a hug.

"We bought fun stuff!" Sadie glowed with happiness.

"I'm going to learn how to jump rope backward like Lindsey does, but we can journal first." Emma gave Sadie a knowing stare. "We're going to be upstairs for a *long* while."

"Uncle Trent?" Noelle tugged on his sleeve.

"What, sweetheart?" She had on her thoughtful expression. He prepared himself for something unexpected.

"I really want some cookies."

He laughed. "Okay. I'll get them."

"I've got it." Gracie held a box of cookies from Annie's Bakery. "Here. Do you have them? Need help carrying them up?"

"Thanks, Gracie. I'm a big girl. I can carry them." Noelle beamed, took the box in both hands and raced out of the room calling, "I've got the cookies!"

Gracie wiped her palms together and gave him a quizzical look. "You're home early."

"Do you mind if we talk for a minute?"

"Sure." She moved toward the kitchen table.

"No, in the living room." He held out his hand, hoping she'd take it. After a skeptical glance, she did. And her small hand felt good in his larger one. He led her to the living room and to the couch. The romantic playlist was coming through the speaker, and he'd lit several candles. Then he tugged her down to sit next to him. "Those are for you."

Her eyes widened at the vase of flowers. "For me?"

"Yeah."

"They're pink."

"Your favorite."

"How did you know?" She leaned forward to smell them. The hope and gratitude in her eyes gave him confidence.

"Your apartment gave it away." He smiled, then shifted, taking her hands in his, and she blinked as she looked into his eyes. "A few weeks ago, you gave me some hard truths. I didn't want to admit you were right." He half expected her to list all the things she'd told him, but she didn't. Her expression told him she was listening and receptive. "But I did what you asked. And it's led me to an unexpected place."

"Where?"

"A place of peace. My job is still important to me. The girls are still important to me. But I'm not worrying all the time. I don't feel like I have to keep tabs on every aspect of my life for it to work out."

"Are you sure? It's only been a few weeks." She sounded curious, not skeptical.

"Yeah, I'm sure. I mean, I might slide back into old habits. I have no idea. But if I do, I know what actions to take to get to a place of peace."

"How?"

"For one, I've been reading the Bible. I've been sitting with my thoughts instead of sitting in front of the television. And I've accepted the lonely parts of my past. Let them go. It's time to move on."

"I'm glad."

"Me, too." He gave her hands a squeeze. "I don't think I ever truly understood God's love until you came along. I was always trying to earn it and coming up short."

"Same here. Still do. Come up short, that is." Her self-deprecating smile was giving him a warm feeling.

"It's okay. I can't be perfect. No one can."

"You really did it, didn't you?" she asked. "Learned to accept yourself. Love yourself."

He nodded. "You were right about that, too. Thank you."

"You're welcome."

"Gracie, I've wanted to take you in my arms for weeks now. I've wanted to tell you all this as it was happening. But something kept holding me back. Today, though, I know it's time."

He was bolstered by the anticipation in her eyes.

"I love you. You could have accepted this job and done the bare minimum. Just sat Noelle on the couch with an iPad and left the girls to their own devices."

"I could never do that." She slipped one hand out of his to press to her chest.

"I know. But a lot of other people could. You really care about the girls. You listen to them, know what they need, you stand up for them, play with them. You're amazing. But that's not why I love you. Well, not the only reason anyway."

She'd grown quiet, vulnerable.

"You're honest with me. Direct. For years, I've been convincing myself I'd have to choose between my career and a girlfriend. But you showed me a different way—one where I could have both. I don't know why you pour so much into me and my nieces, but I'm thankful. And taking this time to figure out who I am and what I'm about? I needed it, but I missed you. I miss everything about what we had before that night with the horse and Sadie."

"I miss it, too."

"I'm sorry I blamed you. Sorry I piled on when I should have been thanking you for all your help. You were the one who calmed Sadie and gave her the comfort she needed."

"I would do the same for any of the girls. Are you sure your feelings for me aren't influenced by my relationship with them?"

"I'm sure. When they go back with their dad, it will be me and maybe Digger. And I'll feel the same about you." He stared into her eyes and took both her hands in his again. "I want to spend more time with you. I want our suppers together and walks to the stables. I want to hear about your day. I can't stand it when you go home without getting a chance to talk to you. I miss you. I love you. Will you please give me a second chance?"

As Gracie looked into his brown eyes, she couldn't quite process that this was the same man who'd accused her of hurting Sadie not long ago. Could she trust this change in him? Or would he revert to a judgmental jerk in the next crisis?

You're sizing him up against people who let you down in the past, and that's not fair.

"I miss our suppers together, too." She did. Ached with longing to have them back. "And I'm glad your faith is stronger. That you've gotten that inner peace."

"But?" His face had fallen as if preparing for her rejection.

But? Did she have a but? Was she ready to move forward? These weeks had helped her clarify things about herself and about Trent. She'd needed time, too.

He was the opposite of the guys she'd dated. He put his nieces' needs above his own. He treated Moulten Stables like he owned it. He was a man who did the right thing, even when it was difficult. When it came down to it, he was pretty selfless.

And she'd realized she'd done the right thing, too, by turning him down. It had been difficult. She'd second-guessed herself almost every day since then.

She really missed what they'd had. Missed their connection. Missed the love that had been growing between them.

As scary as it was to trust that he wouldn't break her heart, it was scarier to live a life of what-ifs. She was ready to take a chance on him.

"I've been reading my Bible, too. And praying. And thinking about what I really want from life."

"You realized it's not me." He hung his head.

"I realized I want a man who loves Jesus, who respects me, who's committed to me, who wants a family."

He stared at her with a shimmer of hope.

"I know this guy who's obsessed with horses. He has a beard, three adorable nieces and a big, rambling farmhouse."

His mouth curved into a smile.

"He's the kind of man who, when he was younger, saw a teenage girl in a vulnerable position and tossed her over his shoulder to take her home. To keep her safe." Her emotions were teetering toward crying. "One who told her that someday she'd realize she was worth more than this. He was right. I was. I am. And I only want you."

He gathered her into his arms and held her so tightly all her worries disappeared. "I don't deserve you, Gracie French."

No one had ever said that to her before. She knew deep down that he meant it.

He searched her eyes. "You really think that about me, don't you? That I'm a good man?"

"I know you are." She ran her hands up his shoulders and slid them behind his neck.

"Okay, here's what I want in a woman." His face looked so much younger when he was happy. "I want a woman who isn't afraid to tell me when I'm wrong, but who will also give me a second chance. I want a woman who respects me, who loves Jesus, who's committed to me. I want a family—three girls would be perfect—and I hope that woman loves a big, rambling farmhouse."

Gracie grinned, nodding at each point.

"I'd like a woman to take on a date on Friday nights. One who insists on pink pillows and plates with bunnies on them. One with the prettiest blond hair I've ever seen, whose big blue eyes light up at just about anything."

"I know a girl like that." She bit the bottom of her lip, hoping he'd kiss her.

"And, for the record, I think your parents and every man in this area were fools for letting you out of their sight. If we'd been closer in age, I would have never let you go."

Her heart. She couldn't stop the tears from forming.

"I love you." He searched her eyes.

"I love you, too."

And then he kissed her.

Everything she'd been through, all of her mistakes, the doubts, the courage, the leap of faith to move here—all combined in this moment to confirm she was exactly where she was supposed to be. In the arms of the man she loved. The one who loved her.

She finally knew what it was like to be cherished, and she'd never let him go.

Chapter Fifteen

Trent drew back from the kiss first. He couldn't believe God had blessed him with this woman. And the sound of footsteps galloping down the stairs had him put a few more inches of distance between him and Gracie. Digger followed the girls and ran straight to where Trent sat on the couch. He picked up the dog and cradled him to his chest while petting him.

"So?" Emma held her arms wide, her eyes round in expectation.

Sadie held her clasped hands under her chin, her eyes wide with hope.

Noelle's bottom lip had plumped out, her eyes watery with unshed tears.

Why was Noelle upset? Maybe the girls had left her out of their journaling or something.

"So, what?" Gracie's face was bright red as she attempted to smooth her hair.

"Are you guys dating?" Emma asked.

Trent figured it was time for him to speak up. "Gracie and I are dating."

"Yippee!" Sadie's arms reached to the sky. Emma was pretending to fan herself. And Noelle promptly began wailing.

He met Gracie's shocked gaze and shrugged. He had no idea what was wrong with the child.

Gracie went over to her and crouched. "What's wrong, Noelle?"

"I wanted you to date my daddy so you could be my mommy!" The words broke throughout, and she sobbed so hard, Trent figured hysterics were sure to follow.

Even Emma and Sadie had stopped their celebrations to look at Noelle with shock.

"Oh, honey, I'm sorry." Gracie drew her into her arms. "That's the sweetest thing anyone's said to me, though. I wish I could be your mommy, too. But I love your uncle."

"Noelle, it will be okay. She's going to be our aunt." Sadie put her arm around Noelle's shoulder.

Whoa. Trent stretched his neck to the side. These girls were getting ahead of themselves.

Gracie tipped her head back and laughed. "We're not quite there yet, girls." She glanced back at him with a smile. "We're just dating."

"But you'll propose to her, right, Uncle Trent?" Emma had her hands on her hips and a determined gleam in her eyes.

"I'd like nothing more than for Gracie to be my wife. But we need to date awhile first."

"Good. It's best to get to know each other." Emma nodded seriously. "Lindsey's mom told her that."

"She's a wise woman." Gracie got to her feet and picked up Noelle. "I love you, you know."

She nodded, resting her cheek on Gracie's shoulder. "I love you, too."

"Now, what do you say we order pizza for supper?" Gracie said. "And then we'll get Digger all leashed up and head over to the stables?"

"Yay!" Emma and Sadie gave each other high fives. "But we have to finish our journals first. Come on, Noelle. We'll help you with yours."

Noelle wiggled for Gracie to let her down, which she did, and the girls ran back upstairs. Digger licked Trent's chin. He laughed, then set him on all fours. The pup raced to the staircase and followed the girls. Gracie came back over and sat next to him.

"Where were we?" Trent slung his arm around her shoulders.

"Ordering a pizza?"

"The pizza can wait." He kissed her again. He couldn't believe she was his. Feminine, kind, strong—the perfect combination. He'd meant what he'd said to Emma. He wanted Gracie to be his wife. To spend forever with her. But…

"What now?" he asked when they ended the kiss.

"Hello? Pizza."

"No, I meant moving forward."

She snuggled into his side. "I like what you said earlier. Friday night dates."

"And supper together?" He curled a lock of her hair around his finger.

"Of course. And walks to the stables."

"And horseback rides."

"Definitely."

"I like this plan."

"I like any plan that includes you."

That's why he loved her. She saw something in him that every other woman had missed. And he'd never take her for granted. He'd been waiting for Gracie French all of his life.

Epilogue

Trent sensed mutiny in the air.

He glanced at Gracie, sitting to his right, at the Jewel River Legacy Club meeting in July. So far, this summer had been the best of his entire life. Emma, Sadie and Noelle were getting suntans from playing outside so much. Emma had taken to horseback riding like a pro. Noelle preferred feeding the horses carrots. And Sadie? Well, he doubted she'd get over her fear of horses, which was a shame.

Angela Zane and Clem Buckley were arguing about something involving a meat locker in town. He didn't even want to know what that was all about. Erica and Dalton Cambridge were trying to get the audiovisual equipment set up. Cade was rolling his eyes at something his mother was saying, and Dean McCaffrey kept checking the clock on the wall.

"Are you sure we needed to be here?" Gracie whispered.

"Trust me on this." At the moment, he was anything but sure—however, he knew how Jewel River worked. "It will be better this way."

"I think we're ready." Erica signaled to Dalton to hit the lights, and the room went dark. Everyone turned their attention to the screen.

"Three years. Three Shakespeare plays. Three productions like you've never seen before." The low male voice paused for a crack of thunder. A banner rippled across the screen with *Taming of the Shrew* written on it. "Prepare to have your minds blown." Dynamite exploded on the screen and digital flames burned up the banner. "If this shrew can't be tamed, she will be thrown into Jewel River." Janey Denton, in costume, stood at the edge of the river. "But Katherina won't go quietly. Will her ninja skills protect her from Petruchio? Or will a cyclone threaten them all?"

Lars Denton, also in costume, approached Janey, who crouched and swept her leg around, tripping him. Then the screen cut to a prairie with a tornado whirling and lightning coming out of the dark sky.

"Jewel River Park. August sixteenth. It's going to be epic." And a series of explosions ended it.

As Dalton flipped the lights back on, Erica stood with a stunned expression. "I didn't realize Joey added ninja kicks to the script."

Angela beamed. "Oh, yes, he said it added drama."

"It adds confusion." Clem shook his head, making a sucking sound with his teeth. "What was wrong with the original?"

"It's more exciting this way, Clem." Angela didn't seem offended. "You never know what you're going to get with one of Joey's productions."

"We'd better not get rabies this year," Clem said.

Cade lifted his finger. "Mackenzie checked all of those raccoons. No one got rabies."

Trent vaguely remembered hearing about the raccoon incident from the previous summer.

"I hope they learned their lesson," Clem said. "They'd better leave all the wild animals at home."

Angela began arguing with Clem, and Erica quickly

brought the meeting back to order. Finally, Erica asked if anyone had any announcements, and Trent stood up.

"I have one." He smiled down at Gracie. "We both do."

Erica smiled and nodded for him to continue.

"I proposed to Gracie this weekend, and she accepted." He helped her to her feet and put his arm around her shoulders. "Thought you'd all like to hear it from us first."

A cheer went up, and Clem came over and congratulated Trent. Then he turned to Gracie. "Well, Goldie, you've got yourself a good man here."

"Thank you, Clem." She blushed. "I couldn't agree more."

"What's going to happen to those girls?" he asked.

"Their father will be finished with his assignment in February." Her face fell. "We'll have to give them back."

"That's too bad." He turned to Trent. "You did good with this one. I'll be over to the stables on Monday."

"Looking forward to it, Clem." Trent still enjoyed their talks. Liked having Clem around.

"All right, Christy, are you going to drive me to Dippity Doo's or what?" Clem marched in Christy Moulten's direction.

"You're going to let *me* drive?" Christy's voice carried. "I thought you said when I parked at the library it was the last time you'd ever get in a vehicle with me behind the wheel."

"I guess I'm living dangerously." The two of them walked toward the door. "You're buying me a hot fudge sundae, by the way..."

Several members stopped by to congratulate them, and finally, Trent ushered Gracie outside to the parking lot where the sun was beginning to set.

"See?" Trent said. "Now everyone knows."

"If they weren't here, they'll know by tomorrow." She

hooked her arm in his as they strolled to his truck. "You know, I've been thinking. About a wedding date."

"Oh, yeah?" He opened the passenger door for her. "What are you thinking? Next week?"

"No, Trent." She slapped his stomach with the back of her hand. "What about next February? When your brother's back? The girls could be in the wedding."

"And Kevin could be my best man." He nodded. "I like it."

"Good. I'll start planning it." Before she could climb into the truck, he held her hand and spun her toward him.

"Whatever you want, whenever you want it—I'll make it happen."

Her mouth curved into a grin. "Dippity Doo's sounds good."

"Done. But first…" He wrapped his arms around her and lifted her off her feet. Then he kissed her. He didn't want it to ever end. He'd found the love of a lifetime, and he planned on holding on to her forever.

* * * * *

If you enjoyed this Wyoming Legacies story,
be sure to pick up the previous books in
Jill Kemerer's miniseries:

The Cowboy's Christmas Compromise
United by the Twins
Training the K-9 Companion
The Cowboy's Christmas Treasures

Available now from Love Inspired!

Dear Reader,

As soon as I started writing this book, I felt bad for Trent—a dedicated man out of his comfort zone—and I breathed a sigh of relief when Gracie took over with the girls. Emma, Sadie and Noelle had been through so much, and I hated to think of them being lost and confused in a strange place. I loved how loyal they were to each other, even as they argued as siblings do.

Gracie had many regrets about her past, but she'd matured and learned to lean on God. I admire how she told Trent that he needed to love himself before he could ever love her. How often we fool ourselves into settling for relationships with people who could take us or leave us. It takes courage to trust in God's best for our lives.

I hope you enjoyed this book in the Wyoming Legacies series. I love connecting with readers. Feel free to email me at jill@jillkemerer.com or write me at P.O. Box 2802, Whitehouse, Ohio, 43571.

Blessings to you!
Jill Kemerer